BAD BEHAVIOR
in the
WORKPLACE
A CAREER IN JEOPARDY

MICHAEL WEINER, MD

BAD BEHAVIOR IN THE WORKPLACE: A CAREER IN JEOPARDY

1210 SW 23rd PL • Ocala, FL 34471 • Phone 352-622-1825
Website: www.atlantic-pub.com • Email: sales@atlantic-pub.com
SAN Number: 268-1250

Library of Congress Control Number: 2022923153

Printed in the United States

PROJECT MANAGER: Crystal Edwards
INTERIOR LAYOUT AND JACKET DESIGN: Nicole Sturk

REVIEWS

While anger, temper and bad behavior may seem to be an anomaly in the world of health care, the reality contradicts this untenable belief.

Health care providers constantly confront frustrations hard to comprehend insurance restrictions, regulatory obstacles rules, regulations, unending paperwork, electronic medical records, disease, death, and financial restrictions. These unending requirements, often impede a caregiver's ability to devote their time and efforts to healing patients who entrust their well-being to these dedicated health professionals.

If one now considers shifting attitudes and mores, one only needs to look at the pandemic, where at the beginning heath care workers were celebrated for their heroism, with parades, sirens, applause, tributes, free meals, only to see that evaporate and be replaced by vicious physical attacks, verbal abuse and anger directed at those very same recent heroes. There is only one conclusion, Dr. Andrew Brown's story is not unique and unusual.

It is all too common that the demands, pressures, disappointments of our health care system precipitates frustration, anger, and bad behavior, however, that doesn't mean it is acceptable, it is not. The challenge for the healthcare industry as depicted by Andrew's story is the desire to possess the courage to change. It is a story worth reading and a lesson worth emulating.

BARRY FREEDMAN
Chief Executive Officer,
Albert Einstein Healthcare System

Dr. Weiner's brilliantly written book about learning and growth is remarkable. Dr. Brown has learned that the norms of workplace behavior have changed and behavior, tolerated years ago, may no longer be accepted. To learn and grow from his behavior is not an easy path for Dr. Brown. But, Dr. Brown has learned, survived and, undoubtedly, will succeed. In writing this timely book, Dr. Weiner reminds us that not every employee will be as fortunate—we need a system that is fairer and more transparent to employees, including those accused of "bad" behavior in the workplace. Our system requires a better means to educate all employees about how the workplace environment has changed and give employees the tools to adapt.

Thanks for sharing the book. I enjoyed reading it. Looking forward to getting together in January

MARTIN D. EDEL
Co-Chair, Sports Law Practice, & Counsel

CAST OF CHARACTERS

In approximate order of appearance:

ANDREW BROWN, MD

LOUISE AND CLARA MCCANN: Founders, Rose Children's Hospital

LUTHER BOLT AND RANDOLPH MCATEER: Pediatric service directors, Rose Children's Hospital

LAWRENCE ROSE: Chief Executive Officer, Rose Harrison Anderson; Board member, University of New York

JEFF FLACK, MD, PHD: Rockefeller Chair of Pediatrics, Rose Children's Hospital

ANNA VALENCIA: Assistant to Jeff Flack, MD, PhD

CHARLES WILKINSON HAVILAND: Real estate philanthropist

LLOYD AND PAUL GERHARD: Donors to the University of New York

PAUL RICHARDS, MD: Chief of Neonatology, Executive Vice Chair, Rose Children's Hospital

MELISSA MENENDEZ, MD: Vice Chair for faculty development, Rose Children's Hospital

CARLOS GUERRERO: Head of Pediatrics Human Resources, Rose Children's Hospital

LUCINDA RODRIQUEZ, MARGARET, and **MAYA:** Spouse and daughters of Carlos Guerrero

FRED MORRIS, MD: Division Director Pediatric Oncology, Rose Children's Hospital

SHALA AHMAD: Administrative director, pediatric oncology, Rose Children's Hospital

BARRY STEINGLASS, MD: Chief Medical Officer, Executive Vice President, University of New York

ALICE: Brown family springer spaniel

OLIVIA SMITH, MD: Dean of Academic Affairs, University of New York

MARISSA BROWN: Spouse of Andrew Brown

CHARLIE MARTIN: Andrew Brown's attorney and friend

BRYSON ALISTAIR: Assistant Director of Human Resources, University of New York

DARA KLEIN: Ombudsman, University of New York

PIA: Andrew Brown's daughter

WILL: Andrew Brown's grandson

CLARA: Andrew Brown's granddaughter

SERGE: Andrew Brown's son

JOHN: Pia's husband and Andrew Brown's son-in-law

GINNIE PARVICH, PHD: Director of Clinical Psychology, and Andrew Brown's therapist

PETER: Marissa Brown's father, Andrew Brown's father-in-law

JANET: Marissa Brown's mother, Andrew Brown's mother-in-law

MITCHELL PRESS: Owner, Camp Echo Sky

DON CAREY: Head counselor, Camp Echo Sky

RUTH BROWN: Andrew Brown's mother

NATHAN BROWN: Andrew Brown's father

MARGARET ("MAGGIE"): Andrew Brown's sister

JAYLEN SAGE: Marissa Brown's sister and business partner

NANCY SAGE: Marissa Brown's sister and business partner

J & N SAGE: Name of the jewelry company owned by Jaylen, Nancy, and Marissa

LOUIS and **CHRIS GOODSPELL:** Owners of Goodspell, Columbus, Ohio

GARY POMERANTZ, MD: Head of Pediatric Oncology, Nationwide Children's Hospital

ARNOLD BROWN: Andrew Brown's uncle and Nathan's brother

BETH: Andrew Brown's cousin

STERGIOS DIMUTRI, PHD: Neurobiologist

GAIL CONNORS: Charge nurse, procedure suite

ATHENA: Stergios Dimutri's twin sister

CHRISTOS: Stergios Dimutri's father

NIKOS: Stergios Dimutri's brother

CONSTANTINE DIMUTRI, MD: Stergios Dimutri's brother

KENNETH ERICSON: Nobel laureate and Stergios Dimutri's mentor

LIANA AKHLAMATHI, DDS: Iranian expatriate and Stergios Dimutri's wife

RICH WILSON: Department of Pediatrics' Chief Financial Officer

BILL SUGARLAND: Director, Course for Distressed Physicians, Carter Singer University

MIKE LAWRENCE, PHD: Instructor, Course for Distressed Physicians, Carter Singer University

GUY WORLEY, MD: Psychiatrist, Course for Distressed Physicians, Carter Singer University

BETH WHITE, MD: Associate Dean of Faculty Affairs, Carter Singer University

BRUCE TYLER, MD: Heart surgeon, Pittsburgh, PA

BRIAN HAMILTON, MD: Urologist, Birmingham, AL

ALAN CHISHOLM, MD: Psychiatrist, Dublin, OH

MICHAEL SMITH, MD: Cardiologist, Ann Arbor, MI

ARNIE SILVER, MD: Andrew Brown's medical school mentor

DR. X: Previous participant, Course for Distressed Physicians

DR. A: Dr. X's colleague, Chair of Medicine

DR. Y: Dr. X's colleague, Associate medical school dean

DR. Z: Dr. X's colleague, Chief Medical Officer

MARY RODRIQUEZ: Director of Nursing, Rose Children's Hospital

EVAN GREEN, MD: Chair for Department of Surgery, University of New York

TABITHA: Serge Brown's wife and Andrew Brown's daughter-in-law

LAWRENCE SHINE, MD: Ginnie Parvich's husband

MAYA SHINE: Ginnie Parvich's daughter

MAILA and **ADELAIDE DIMUTRI:** Stergios and Liani Dimutri's daughters

JACKIE LEWIS: Pediatric Oncologist, Rose Children's Hospital

CASEY DOYLE: Pediatric Oncologist, Rose Children's Hospital

CHERYL KANG: Pediatric Oncologist, Rose Children's Hospital

MARIE ABRUZZO: Pediatric Oncologist, Rose Children's Hospital

ARTHUR CHARLES: Internist, Andrew Brown's personal physician

CORRINE, BETH, ANGELA, MAYRA: Outpatient nurses, Pediatric Oncology

KIM: Nurse Practitioner, Pediatric Oncology

ARTHUR CHARLES: Andrew Brown's internist

JOANNA: Phlebotomist, Pediatric Oncology Ambulatory Center

PATTY PARISI: Charge nurse, Pediatric Oncology

ANDREA ROGNOLIA: Nursing administration, Rose Children's Hospital

GLADYS GALLAGHER: Director of Human Resources, Rose Children's Hospital

WILHELM ROSTOKOVICH: Professor of Archeology

GUSTAVE MARANZINI: Professor of Classical History

MIKE: Manager, Blue Eagle Moving Company

LUCIA CARMELLA: Deceased patient, family owns Carmella's restaurant

GARY SHEFFIELD: local Hudson Valley mover

MARGARET QUINN: Store Manager, Goodwill

RICH CARLISLE: Andrew Brown's friend; President, Alpine Palisade Capital Management

GIL VINCENT: Director of Personal Wealth Management, Alpine Palisade Capital Management

WILLIAM FISKE: Presidential scholar; Chairperson, American History Department, Barth College

VIJAY SATAWAR, MD: Chief of Pediatric Oncology, Albany Medical Center, Hudson Valley Memorial

MAHESH GHOSH, MD: Chair of Pediatrics, Hudson Valley Memorial

RANJIV CUTERA, MD: Director, Volunteers in Medicine

JACK, ARTHUR, BRUCE, BARRY, GARY, JED: Andrew Brown's golf buddies

HAL SHORT, MD: Surgeon, University of New York

JANET AMARO, MD: Andrew Brown's oncologist

ROGER BRITON, MD: Andrew Brown's thyroid specialist

LAURA TEDESCHI, MD: Andrew Brown's dermatologist

TABLE OF CONTENTS

FOREWORD

When I initially began researching this book, my curiosity regarding its subject matter was largely personal. Like the main character of this fictionalized account, I too was a longtime pediatric oncologist who had been recently reprimanded by my institution following an unprofessional outburst in the workplace. It had not been the first time that my inability to regulate my anger had caused issues in my personal or work life, but the repercussions exceeded any that I had previously dealt with. I was nearing the end of my career, and realized that while the culture around me had changed, I had failed to change with it.

This was a difficult period for me, both personally and professionally. In many ways, I felt adrift and worried that the legacy I had worked to establish over the course of many decades might be overshadowed by these personal failings. I had two options: Either I could remain stagnant, clinging to the patterns of behavior that had failed me in the past, or I could treat these setbacks as an opportunity for growth.

I was curious about anger's place in history and its manifestations in culture, art, and literature, as well as in the workplace. I felt that a deeper dive into the origins of anger might help me to better understand both my own relationship with anger and its role in our culture. Therefore, I devoted a chapter to a brief history of anger through recorded time. Additionally, I discussed the presence of an "anger gene" and the pros and cons of anger, temper, and rage. Ultimately, I hoped that my research would allow me to move into this next phase of my life in a more productive and receptive way.

Upon beginning my task, I was faced with several central and open-ended questions. Perhaps the most foundational of these was whether anger could somehow be a positive trait. I recognized that my own tendencies toward anger largely stemmed from a desire for control. Although through outbursts of rage, I was often able to regain some sense of control, it was predicated on fear rather than respect and was therefore difficult to maintain. I was curious whether it was possible for expressions of anger, if demonstrated with more restraint, to have any productive value. In considering this question, I turned to ancient mythology, religion, and literature. I researched the anger of the Greek gods and the Hebrew God, as well as its manifestation by contemporary political and cultural figures. Additionally, I considered the possible existence of an "anger gene" of some sort that would predispose certain people toward acts of anger.

I wove my research into the story of Andrew Brown, a pediatric oncologist at the fictional University of New York, who must navigate his institution's bureaucratic human resource structures after a disruptive incident of anger in the workplace.

Through the character of Andrew Brown, I was able to revisit some of the most difficult and painful incidents of anger in my own past. Andrew is committed to improving his behavior, and works closely with a therapist. Together, the two revisit inciting incidents in Brown's past to better understand his current mental state. In addition to their personal therapy sessions, the two engage in a broader research project regarding anger that closely mirrors my own.

While much of my research remained inconclusive, the value of the work lay in its process. There may very well be an anger gene—there certainly is evidence to support its existence—however, untangling the indications of that gene from childhood conditioning and situational triggers would be difficult, if not impossible. Moreover, the treatment and management of anger likely would not change. While selective serotonin reuptake inhibitors (SSRIs) or other medications might help individuals to regulate their behavior, the treatment for most moderate cases would continue to be behavioral modification.

With Andrew Brown's story, my hope is not necessarily to answer whether anger has positive effects or whether a genetic predisposition toward it exists, but rather to reach out to others who are similarly struggling. Through my main character, I hope to demonstrate that behavior modification is possible at any stage of life or career through hard work and perseverance. And, more so, I hope to show those who struggle with anger that they are not alone.

CHAPTER 1

ADMINISTRATIVE HOLD

It was a stifling day in early August, with temperatures in the mid-90s and heavy, languid humidity. ConEd had reduced power output citywide by 10 percent to meet the increased demand for electricity, and the straining window box AC units in the old buildings of the University of New York Medical School were terribly insufficient.

The air in Andrew Brown's small corner office on the fourth floor of the Powell Ambulatory Building was stagnant. A portable desk fan was noisily circulating the oppressive heat like a miniature convection oven. This was Brown's fourth office at the Rose Children's Hospital since his return 25 years prior. It was also his favorite. It was small for certain, perhaps 100 square feet, but it held everything he needed—two bookshelves replete with mementos and personal artifacts nestled among the books, a desk with return, and a wall-mounted cabinet were all he really needed. The blue linoleum floor was covered by a black and gray area rug made of recycled plastic bottles.

Atop it stood a sturdy desk with two modern task lamps purchased at the Museum of Modern Art store. Brown rarely used the overhead fluorescent lights. No diplomas adorned the walls. Instead, he'd hung two framed items: a photo of Barack Obama and a *New York Times Magazine* issue whose featured story on brain function and memory included a cover photo of his former patient, Kathy Jennings. Behind the desk, the large window overlooked a bustling Hamilton Avenue. The office was perfect.

The University of New York Medical School, one of the oldest schools in the country, was founded in 1765 as Queens and Kings College by virtue of a charter from King George III. After the Revolutionary War, the college had adopted its present name, and the school of medicine was integrated into the larger university. Today, the schools of medicine, nursing, and public health and the university hospital occupy a sprawling conglomeration of buildings in northern Manhattan.

The Rose Children's Hospital, formerly the Infants' and Children's Hospital, was founded by sisters Louise and Clara McCann in 1890, and originally occupied a brownstone on the West Side of Manhattan. The dedicated facility for ill children was the first of its kind in New York City and the fourth in the country, following similar hospitals in Philadelphia, Boston, and Cincinnati. During the Depression years of the 1920s and 1930s, the hospital relocated to the University of New York's campus and administratively and financially merged with the parent institution.

The Infants' and Children's Hospital has a long, storied history of leadership, discovery, and innovation. Two of the early pediatric service directors, Luther Bolt and Randolph McAteer, were among the small, distinguished group of doctors responsible for advancing the subspecialty of pediatrics nationally, each authoring authoritative texts considered to be the gold standard in the field at the time. Early hospital luminaries created programs in child neurology, radiology, pathology, and neonatology that were among the first such programs in the country. Faculty members, many of whom were women, were the first to describe celiac disease, establish a scoring system for newborn vitality, introduce antibiotic use to combat bacterial infections, and perform the first successful heart transplant in a child.

The Rose Children's Hospital acquired its name to memorialize the significant contributions of Lawrence Rose, the chief executive officer of the financial services firm Rose Harrison Anderson, and a member of the board of directors of the University of New York. Lawrence, the grandson of Herbert Rose, a Wall Street scion and founder of the firm, was also a graduate of the University of New York and was involved as a patron and humanitarian of the university for more than thirty years. The Rose family philanthropy was transformative for the university, but it was the personal contributions from Lawrence and his colleagues at the firm that would forever link his family's name with the hospital.

Andrew Brown was proud to be a member of the department of pediatrics at RCH and the University of New York. He worked hard, paid his dues, and achieved his position through honesty and sincerity. He always put his patients first, and the interests and careers of his colleagues above his own. The formula worked. He had enjoyed a long, satisfying career and had the respect and admiration of both university and hospital leadership.

One afternoon, Andrew was reviewing emails, although daydreaming more than truly absorbing the information, when his mobile phone rang.

"Dr. Brown, it's Anna Valencia. Dr. Flack wants to see you immediately. Are you available?"

"Sure, what's it about?" He was curious—why would the chair of pediatrics want to speak with him so urgently?

"He didn't say. He just asked me to call and ask you to come up."

Impromptu urgent calls were never good. Brown loathed going to meetings, but he especially hated going into one without knowing its purpose. His heart rate quickened.

Perhaps he was being summoned for something positive, a new project or task, he reasoned. But that scenario seemed unlikely. He racked his brain. As far as he could recall, he had neither said nor done anything wrong. Nevertheless, the uncertainty unnerved him. He left his office, locked the door, and slowly trudged to the chairman's office suite on the 12th floor of the old university hospital building, now converted to academic offices.

When Dr. Brown had joined the faculty several decades prior, the university hospital building housed inpatient floors for Medicaid patients, the indigent, and the uninsured—mostly from the surrounding neighborhood.

The units had open wards, multiple-patient rooms, and shared bathrooms, which offered little to no privacy. Antiquated operating rooms, obstetrical delivery rooms, and the diagnostic radiology suite had occupied the 3rd, 4th, and 5th floors, respectively. Patients were cared for by interns and residents and rarely saw an attending physician. The physical facility was suboptimal, and delivery of care was only nominally better than Third World medicine.

Insured private patients from affluent neighborhoods in Manhattan, New Jersey, and Westchester County were cared for in the Haviland Pavilion, named for Charles Wilkinson Haviland, a wealthy real estate magnate and philanthropist who also gave a gift to name the Eye and Ear Institute at the University of New York. All rooms were private with en suite bathrooms. Every floor had a solarium. The dietary service prepared meals to order from a large menu, which often included filet mignon and prime rib. When patients arrived for admission, they were provided monogrammed bathrobes and slippers. Every patient had a knowledgeable and experienced senior faculty member to privately manage their care. The Haviland Pavilion rivaled the Ritz-Carlton or Four Seasons in amenities and service.

The disparity in the treatment provided for rich and poor, white and people of color was stark.

This chasm of care narrowed in the mid-1990s with the construction of the new Gerhard Hospital Building. The old university hospital building was converted to administrative offices for the clinical departments, computer labs, information technology offices, and a modern ambulatory dental clinic and school. The Haviland Pavilion was closed and the space converted to psychiatric offices, faculty practice physician office suites, hospital laboratories, transfusion suites, the department of rehabilitation and regenerative medicine, and Workforce Health and Safety, or employee healthcare.

The Gerhard Hospital was a 1,000-bed facility without discriminatory separation of patients—rather, they were aggregated by diagnosis. There were individual units for patients with cancer, heart disease, and neurological disorders, sections for general medicine and general surgery, units for subspecialty surgery, new operating rooms, diagnostic radiology, and several technologically advanced intensive care units. Care was rendered to all patients by hospitalists, residents, and senior attending physicians who were ever-present, making twice-daily rounds on all patients. The entire enterprise, while imperfect and still largely dependent on unequal medical insurance coverage, was a dramatic improvement over that of the '90s.

Dr. Jeff Flack had recently been appointed the eighth Rockefeller Chair of Pediatrics in the history of the Rose Children's Hospital. He was relatively young for a department chair and Pediatrician in Chief, having just celebrated his 50th birthday. His age, however, belied his extraordinary accomplishments and career. He had graduated from the MD-PhD program at Yale University, where he'd also been a top-ranked lacrosse player. He completed his training at Boston Children's and Children's Hospital of Philadelphia, where he remained on faculty until he was recruited to Children's Hospital of Los Angeles to serve as both Director of Pulmonology and head of the research enterprise. His work on the immune function of the lungs was groundbreaking, and he had received numerous accolades, including his induction into the prestigious Academy of Medicine.

Brown remembered the first time he'd met Jeff Flack. He had been in the department executive suite with Paul Richards, Chief of Neonatology and Executive Vice Chair, and Melissa Menendez, Vice Chair for Faculty Development. They had recently concluded a vice chairs meeting and Flack had requested an introductory meeting. Flack introduced himself, greeted each of them individually by name, and said, "Let me tell you a little bit about myself."

He'd told them that he was a native New Yorker, raised in Roslyn on the North Shore of Long Island. His father, an accountant, had died prematurely from a heart attack, and his mother managed a jewelry boutique on the Miracle Mile in Manhasset. He and his wife, Carolyn, a physical therapist, had met in Philadelphia and had three sons. Flack's demeanor was unique, to say the least. He was direct and transparent, if somewhat lacking in traditional gentility. But Andrew and his colleagues found it refreshing.

He kept the conversation personal, asking each of them about their families and where they lived.

Andrew couldn't help thinking about how well their first meeting had gone as he apprehensively approached the man's office now.

"Hi, Dr. Brown. I'll let Dr. Flack know you're here," the assistant said, disappearing behind the office door.

"Thanks, Anna."

Almost immediately, the door to Jeff Flack's office reopened and Andrew was ushered inside.

Flack's office was large and tastefully decorated. Ten-foot ceilings, a marble floor, and north- and east-facing windows with spectacular views of the city skyline were complemented by an elliptical mahogany desk tucked into the corner, upon which sat four massive computer screens, reminding Andrew of a control room for a space station. There was a seating area with a glass table in the center, two chairs, and a small sofa in front of a large screen with bookshelves on either side. Hanging on the walls were the obligatory diplomas and framed awards.

Flack rose from where he sat and gestured. "Come in, Andrew—have a seat. I've asked Carlos to join us."

Carlos Guerrero was the head of the department's human resources office. Andrew had known him for decades and had worked with him often on new hires and recruits. They had a good working relationship and a mutual respect for one another. But his presence did not bode well.

Andrew took a seat on the sofa across from where Flack and Carlos sat in the chairs.

Flack began by telling him that this was the most difficult and uncomfortable professional conversation he had ever had. "I want you to know that you are a friend, colleague, and valued member of the department," he assured Andrew. "Your importance and imprint on your division and the department are immeasurable. I am grateful for all you do." He paused and took a deep breath. "But I'm afraid I have no choice…I have to put you on administrative hold."

There was a roaring in Andrew's ears. He was speechless, his mind racing. "What? Administrative hold? I don't even know what that is—what do you mean? What have I done?" The knot in his stomach tightened. This was worse than he had imagined.

"A complaint has been lodged, and it has to be investigated," Guerrero explained, not unkindly. "During the investigation, your hospital privileges will be temporality suspended—that means no patient care."

"You'll, of course, continue to receive your full biweekly salary," Flack quickly interjected.

Andrew sat stupefied for a moment. "And what am I meant to do during this? I'm supposed to go on inpatient service next week. There are people out on vacation—I have responsibilities—patients and families counting on me!" He paused, the reality of the situation beginning to dawn on him. "What was this complaint? What am I possibly meant to have done?"

Flack kept his tone conciliatory but firm. "I'm sorry, but we're required to keep the details of the complaint private until the investigation has been completed." He might as well have been reading from an HR manual. "Take some time off. Give it a few days, maybe a week or so. Hopefully we'll get to the other side quickly."

Andrew was beside himself. "How can you do this without even letting me know what I'm being charged with?"

"No one is charging you with anything," Flack said patiently. To Andrew, the placating words were steeped in condescension.

Carlos suggested Andrew look through the hospital bylaws. "There's information in there about the process and your rights—"

"Who all knows about this? This is outrageous!" Brown interrupted.

"Fred Morris and Shala Ahmad, the division director and administrator— no one else. Barry Steinglass is directing the investigation for the hospital.

"Who is he?"

Guerrero explained that Steinglass was the chief medical officer and an executive vice president at the hospital. He had been an anesthesiologist and director of the operating rooms, but was now an administrator with an unenviable responsibility.

Flack stood and hugged Brown in an out-of-character display of affection.

"Just relax and enjoy some paid time off," he said encouragingly. "You'll get through this."

And with that, the meeting was over.

Andrew Brown walked slowly back to his office in disbelief. His head was filled with fear, anger, and chaos. Even his questions had questions. As he looked around his office, he reminded himself that there was nothing here he was allowed to do. Andrew shut down his computer, turned off the fan and task lights, straightened the papers on his desk, and packed his attaché case with what he thought he might need. Still in shock, he put on his blue blazer and locked the door to the office he loved so dearly. He took the elevator to the lobby and walked out of the building. It was 3 o'clock in the afternoon when he unlocked the door to his apartment in Dobbs Ferry. His wife, Marissa, was not home, but Alice, their springer spaniel, met him at the door enthusiastically.

After taking Alice for a walk, Andrew went upstairs to his home office, opened his laptop, and sent Barry Steinglass an email requesting an explanation and asking if there was anything he could do.

Steinglass did not reply.

Two days, then three, passed without response. He was in limbo, floundering without recourse. Andrew called Steinglass's office, and his assistant said he was on vacation and would be out for two weeks.

Although Flack was supportive, he had no information to share. Andrew thought it highly unlikely Flack did not know what he'd allegedly done, but he was not forthcoming. Flack simply repeated that he was "not at liberty to discuss the situation" and politely refused to budge.

Andrew asked if there was any chance he would come through this ordeal in one piece, but Flack's reply was nebulous, cagey. "Be patient," was his only offer. He suggested Andrew contact Olivia Smith, dean of academic affairs at the University of New York. But it was August, and Dean Smith was also on vacation and would not be returning until the 21st.

CHAPTER 2

WAITING IN LIMBO

Andrew felt humiliated, like a child who was being reprimanded though he didn't even know the parameters of his discretion. The situation remained stagnant.

Days passed.

Then a week.

Then two, with no communication—just silence. Andrew began to wonder if he would ever hear back or if this limbo would drag on forever. He was plagued by a low-grade anxiety that clung to him like an unwelcome shadow from the moment he opened his eyes in the morning until he fell into a restless, fitful sleep at night.

It was Dr. Brown's routine to give his cell numbers to the parents of his patients. Their calls were few, but it was an important step in gaining their trust. Being available to answer questions and allay fears as they arose, rather than the next day or after the weekend, was important to him and to his patients.

Only a short time into his absence from work, he began to hear from his patients. They wanted to know if he was all right and why he was not in the clinic rendering care. He had no answers, so he simply reassured them that he was well.

Marissa attempted to be an accessible, helpful resource to her husband, but she had no real answers. When he first told her the news, she was just as outraged and distraught as he was—however, his tendency to obsess was wearing her patience thin. Andrew was like a dog with a bone. Over and over, he returned to his conversation with Flack, mining its sparse details for some new revelation that might help him to understand how he, a well-respected, scrupulous professional, could possibly have arrived at his current predicament. Marissa, the unhappy recipient of these monologues, remained calm but worried as her husband continued to unravel under the weight of his anxieties. All the while, there was still no word from anyone about anything. His sojourn in limbo dragged on.

Andrew contacted Charlie Martin, an attorney and friend. They had met on a recent Holland Fitch group tour of Southeast Asia that included visits to Hanoi, Saigon, the ruins of Angkor Wat, the Imperial Palace, and the outdoor markets and canals of Bangkok. The trip was fantastic, and for three weeks, the Martins and Browns had been inseparable. They had bonded immediately, had similar families—an older daughter and a son—and similar interests in politics, sports, and food. Charlie, a graduate of Columbia University and Harvard Law School, was a managing director at Levin Smith Colson, a modestly sized firm with offices in New York, Boston, and Chicago. His area of expertise was employment law, so Andrew was hopeful his friend would have some helpful advice.

Charlie agreed with Andrew that the actions of the University of New York were highly unusual and probably contrary to generally accepted guidelines and principles of human resources. An administrative timeout during an investigation without informing the alleged wrongdoer of the allegations seemed fundamentally wrong. Charlie was quick to point out that conversations around racism and sexism in the workplace were leading to important shifts in the field of human resources. Andrew agreed, acknowledging the importance of protecting accusers against retribution. Still, to leave the accused so fully in the dark seemed inappropriate and contrary to his own rights. If he was, indeed, innocent until proven guilty, then why was the hospital treating him like an active threat, too dangerous even to be informed of his wrongdoing?

Charlie and Andrew discussed writing a letter to Flack and Steinglass, but ultimately decided to temporize, at least for the moment. Instead, Charlie suggested that Andrew keep exhaustive notes documenting every conversation, email, message, and thought related to the issue.

The following Monday, two full weeks after the original meeting with Flack, Steinglass finally responded to Andrew's email. He apologized for the delay, explaining that he had been out of the country on vacation with limited internet access. He assured Andrew that he would get up to speed quickly and would get back to him with the path forward as soon as he had information. Dean Smith similarly contacted Andrew and made an appointment to speak that Wednesday.

Finally—movement. A good thing certainly, but Andrew still had no answers. He emailed Flack, who told him the investigation, whatever that might be, was a priority. Flack responded that he was hopeful it would not take much longer. The end was in sight.

Charlie Martin agreed. Be patient.

Olivia Smith was one of six vice or associate deans at the University of New York Medical Center. Smith's role was to assist faculty in navigating the complex bureaucratic system of one of the leading academic medical centers in the country. Dean Smith was a practicing pulmonologist and worked at the community health center two days a week, caring for patients with asthma and chronic obstructive pulmonary disease as a result of tobacco use.

Arriving for his meeting on Wednesday, Andrew took in his surroundings. Olivia Smith's cluttered first-floor office was nondescript—a desk, some bookshelves, piles of papers strewn everywhere. The organization system was one known only to Olivia. But there was one notable object—a signed photograph from President Barack Obama: "To Dr. Olivia Smith, thank you for your service." Seeing the photo, Brown couldn't help but feel a pang, remembering his beloved office and his own framed photo of the former president.

Dean Smith, a woman of color, hailed from the South Side of Chicago. She had graduated from Northwestern and the University of Chicago Medical School, quickly rising in the professional ranks. She had befriended First Lady Michelle Obama, and together they had worked on developing healthcare policy for the underprivileged youth of the Second City. When Barack Obama was elected president, she served his administration as a healthcare expert and was instrumental in formulating provisions for the Affordable Care Act. After her stint in Washington, she was recruited as an associate dean at the University of New York, where she developed the university's policies on diversity and inclusion.

As he took a seat, Andrew expressed gratitude to Dean Smith for seeing him during her vacation.

Dean Smith told Andrew that she did not have any new information, but promised she would speak with Jeff Flack and Barry Steinglass to help move the process along. She apologized to Andrew and told him that he was a victim of the summer—August vacations delayed a resolution.

Andrew sighed inwardly in frustration. He couldn't believe his whole future was so obscured in hazy uncertainty. He couldn't walk out of here without at least some small morsel of information.

"Tell me one thing at least..." Andrew broached the topic hesitantly. "I have to know."

He needed to know if he had been accused of some kind of sexual harassment.

She assured him that he had not. Allegations of harassment—anything of a sexual nature—were handled far differently. Olivia told him be patient a bit longer and ended the meeting by promising she'd get to the bottom of this, and soon.

Within days of his meeting with Smith, Andrew received an email from Steinglass and Flack, scheduling a meeting in Flack's office the following

Monday. The investigation had been completed, and the university hospital was ready to present their findings.

Andrew and Charlie Martin considered the necessity of an attorney's presence at the meeting, but they concluded that Martin's presence would be construed as confrontational, and it would be best not to be adversarial. If necessary, there would be time for lawyers in the future, but for now, Charlie wanted Andrew to take copious notes and, if possible, record the conversation if no one objected.

Monday could not come soon enough. Flack, Steinglass, and Smith were all in attendance, as was Bryson Alistair, an assistant director of human resources for the University of New York Hospital. Steinglass, with whom Andrew had only spoken via email and phone, introduced himself, and the two shook hands.

Steinglass was small in stature, but he spoke with authority as he laid out the matter at hand.

There had been multiple complaints filed against Andrew following episodes of broken tempers and angry outbursts.

"Coworkers have stated that your language, including your use of the word 'fuck,' is offensive and inappropriate," Bryson Alistair said.

Andrew sat wordless, lost in incredulity. He struggled silently with himself, fighting the rising urge to react spontaneously. It was imperative that he present a calm demeanor—this meeting was the last place to lose his temper.

He admitted to himself that, yes, on occasion he had lost his temper, and yes, he had sometimes used inappropriate language, but so did many others—this was not unique. It was actually rather common. He worked, day in and day out, with children dying of cancer—this was not a normal job with normal stressors. Was the occasional emotional display not warranted?

Andrew was pissed. He had spent three weeks in limbo, agonizing in uncertainty, and for what?

He closed his eyes, took one deep breath and then another, and reminded himself that this assemblage was not the time or place to defend himself. He could not let his anger get the best of him—he could not prove them right. He sat silent, listening with what he hoped was a stoic expression on his face. He accepted the allegations and took copious notes. He reasoned he would have his chance to speak his mind about the situation, but now was not that time.

The person whose opinion Andrew most cared about was Flack. After all, he was a member of Flack's department, a vice chair for external relations, and he could not risk alienating his boss. He explained that when he did express anger, it was never directed against a coworker or colleague, but rather it was situational. Treating children with cancer and grappling with insurance companies could be maddening, heartbreaking. Might he have lost his temper on behalf of a patient and family who had been denied access to care by an insurance company? Sure. Frustrating predicaments secondary to bureaucracy, a cumbersome healthcare system that did not always put patients first—these were his daily realities. Flack and Dean Smith agreed and expressed their understanding. They apologized for the situation, but the damage was done.

Steinglass informed Andrew that his administrative timeout was over, and his privileges would be immediately reinstated. He could resume patient care and return to his normal routine. Steinglass suggested that he make an appointment to continue their conversation after Labor Day in order to give him some time to process. He again expressed regret at the length of the ordeal.

"August, after all."

Brown decided that the best path forward was contrition. He told the group that he was aware of his temper and vowed to use the episode as a learning experience. He would commit himself to modifying his behavior and altering his tone, recognizing that profanity was unacceptable in the workplace. Frankly, Andrew was so deeply relieved that he would be able to continue the work he prized that he would have said anything.

Flack had one request that was quickly endorsed by all in attendance. He had read about physician programs specifically designed for distressed doctors and suggested that Andrew attend one, assuring him that the department would cover all associated expenses.

After quashing his irritation at the phrase "distressed physician," Andrew agreed to research the options and report back.

Dean Smith suggested that Brown make an appointment with the medical center's ombudsman, Dara Klein, and offered to make an introduction.

Still in a paradoxical state of shock and relief, Andrew Brown thanked Flack, Steinglass, and Smith before dazedly exiting the office and heading outside. Habit drove him in the direction of his office in the Powell Building, but he stopped and slumped onto a bench in the garden at the center of the Medical Center Complex.

He called Marissa, but there was no answer. "Honey, it's over. Be home soon and I'll explain. I'm fine."

Charlie Martin, however, was waiting for his call. "It's over. You won't believe it. The entire ordeal was about the word 'fuck.'"

Charlie laughed. "Explain."

Andrew told him that someone, probably a nurse practitioner in the outpatient clinic, had complained about an outburst he'd had—a momentary lapse of control, a fit of temper—and his use of profanity. They'd claimed that his anger created a less-than-collegial work environment. He recalled an incident in which a newly diagnosed leukemic child was hospitalized at Bronx General, an institution totally unequipped to manage the case. The family requested a transfer to the oncology team at the University of New

York Rose Children's Hospital, but their insurer, a Medicaid managed care program, did not have a contract with the hospital and denied the transfer, despite the willingness of the RCH staff to accept the case.

Andrew told Charlie that he distinctly remembered spending more than an hour trying to cajole the insurance administrators into allowing him to manage the child's care, but to no avail. Upon ending the call, he recalled pounding his fist on the table and proclaiming, "Goddammit! Those fucking bitches!"

It was inappropriate, certainly, but he had allowed the heat of the moment to get the best of him.

Andrew had then spoken directly to the family and had suggested that they self-discharge from Bronx General and come immediately to the emergency department at RCH. He assured the parents their child would not be denied care, regardless of their insurance, and the child would be admitted and receive therapy—no questions asked. He told the parents that he would notify the social work team straightaway and begin converting their insurance into a care program accepted by the University of New York. He told Charlie that he knew how to play the system to overcome the bureaucracy and put his patients first.

Still, he was endlessly frustrated. The additional time and effort required by the staff, not to mention the extra stress the parents experienced, would not be necessary if only people would be reasonable and do what was best for children with cancer and their families.

Charlie agreed, but encouraged Andrew to take a deep breath and try, at least for the time being, to let it go and focus on the positive—he could return to his patients.

That evening, Andrew explained the events of the day to Marissa. She was relieved, if not surprised. They'd been married more than 40 years, and she had witnessed her husband's anger and explosive outbursts. He, of course, had never been violent, but his temper was unnerving, nonetheless. That his anger was the root of the issue came as no shock. She had learned to live with his temper over the years—though she despised it—and while she never would have wished for her husband's work to be compromised, a part of her was glad that he would now have to put in the time and effort to make a substantive change. Andrew had been impossible to handle during his monthlong leave, and Marissa was eager for things to settle down.

Marissa told Andrew that he should learn from the embarrassment and humiliation of the tribulation and take corrective actions. "Change for me, change for your children, change for the well-being of your colleagues, but most importantly, change for yourself."

Andrew told her that Flack wanted him to attend one of the corrective courses for distressed physicians, and that he had agreed to both. Independently, he told his wife—his best friend—that he would engage in individual corrective behavioral modification with a psychologist at the hospital. He also decided to commit himself to studying anger, its origins, underpinnings, etiology, manifestations, and repercussions. He concluded that he had to educate himself if he were to change, and change was imperative.

CHAPTER 3

HARD TO BELIEVE, BUT TRUE

The Labor Day weekend was one of reflection and contemplation for Andrew Brown. He and Marissa went to their Hudson Valley home about 90 miles north of the city to spend the holiday together.

The apartment in Dobbs Ferry was a dwelling of convenience. It was a short commute to the medical center and was close to their daughter, Pia, and grandchildren, Will and Clara. Over the years, Andrew and Marissa had lived in a variety of locations in and around the city, moving periodically to accommodate their family's changing needs. Their first home had been a well-loved but small one-bedroom apartment on Abington Square in Greenwich Village. Its "cozy" size never bothered them, as they had the whole of the Village at their fingertips, but once Pia was born, it became immediately clear that they needed more space. They had then, with the financial assistance of their parents, purchased an eight-room cooperative apartment on East 87th Street close to the Guggenheim. They also purchased a small house in Remsenburg, a hamlet near Westhampton, for the weekends.

After Serge was born and started school, the cost of two mortgages in addition to two private-school tuitions became too great to bear. Marissa and Andrew decided to simplify and consolidate. They sold the apartment and the beach house and moved to Tenafly, New Jersey, a 5-mile commute to the George Washington Bridge. Tenafly was a wonderful community to raise a family, with excellent public schools, eclectic neighborhoods of well-manicured homes, new, yet lasting friendships, soccer, hockey, figure skating for Pia and Serge, and golf at Alpine Country Club for Andrew. It was idyllic. The Browns' center-hall brick colonial home in the Old Smith Village section of town had two fireplaces, a wood-paneled den, a sunroom, and five bedrooms. It was the perfect place to raise a family. However, when the children left the nest, the house felt too big and too expensive. They once again moved—this time to a rental apartment in Hoboken, purchasing their home in Rhinebeck for the weekends.

Hoboken, famous as the birthplace of Frank Sinatra, was fantastic. The Browns' two-bedroom, ninth-floor apartment had floor-to-ceiling windows and an unobstructed view of the spectacular Manhattan skyline, directly across the Hudson River from the Empire State Building. The panorama was perhaps one of the best cityscapes in the world, and it was right outside their living room window. Hoboken was similar to the Village, with busy streets, an abundance of good restaurants, and a spectacular, glorious Riverwalk that stretched the entire length of the city, between Secaucus and Jersey City. They had loved it. But when Pia and John moved to Westchester with their two children, the trip to come visit became tedious. The move to Dobbs Ferry was just one of expediency, but it seemed to work.

The Rhinebeck house was their retreat—a place for calm deliberation. The Browns considered it their permanent residence, and every time they drove through the quaint surrounding village to get to their weekend retreat, a sense of calm settled over them.

Saturday morning, Andrew played a round of golf with friends at Old Forge Golf Club in neighboring Germantown but was too preoccupied with the events of the week to concentrate on his game and wound up losing a few bucks. Pia, John, and the children arrived Saturday afternoon for swimming, fishing, and a holiday barbecue of hamburgers and hot dogs. Their company was a welcome distraction, though not entirely effective. Andrew's mind was still on the events of the week before. He sent emails to Dara Klein, the ombudsman, and Dr. Ginnie Parvich, a highly recommended psychologist in the University's Psychiatric Institute, asking when they might have time to meet in person. Despite the holiday weekend, they both replied quickly and offered to make time to meet with him that Tuesday.

The rest of the weekend passed in a blur for Andrew.

Dara Klein's first-floor office was at 168 Hamilton Avenue, a nondescript edifice several blocks north of the Powell Ambulatory Building. Late Tuesday afternoon, Andrew made his way to the ombudsman's office. The streets were crowded with scores of students returning after the summer recess, and excitement was in the air with the new academic year about to begin. He pressed the buzzer for Suite 104 and stepped into the building's lobby. Klein greeted him at her office door.

"Come in, Dr. Brown. Pleased to meet you," she said, cordially extending a hand.

"Please, call me Andrew."

"Only if you call me Dara."

As she ushered him into her office, she told Andrew that she had been a practicing defense attorney at Tate Iverson, a well-known New York City law firm, where her specialty had been white-collar crime. She had resigned from the grind to spend more time at home with her husband and children after the family had dealt with several health issues. Dara and Olivia Smith had become friends through their work, so when the dean called to ask if she wanted to establish an ombudsman's office at the University of New York, she saw it as the perfect opportunity to return to the workforce part-time. Dara viewed her role as one of support for faculty and university staff to confidentially resolve internal issues raised by members of the community.

Having spoken with Dean Smith, Dara was familiar with the allegations that had been levied against Andrew. She explained that, given the fact that his path forward had already been agreed upon, her own role was largely curtailed. Andrew asked Dara to explain the decision to keep the name or names of the accusers anonymous. He explained that he would like to apologize, recognizing that his outburst and profanity were toxic and inappropriate. She explained to him that the reasoning boiled down to protection.

"People need to feel safe in speaking freely without fear of retribution."

"I understand that," Andrew said. "I know anonymity is a fundamentally important principle in situations where reprisal is likely, but I can't help but be troubled by the lack of transparency here."

He reasoned that what might be considered egregious behavior by one individual could just as easily be construed by others as normal, not unusual, part of the conversation.

"Excuse my French, Dara, but 'fuck' is part of the vernacular. I'm shocked that its utterance might rise to the level of potentially altering one's career."

"Dr. Brown, I agree that what is perceived as bad behavior by some is considered routine and non-offensive by others," said Dara. "But while I don't know all of the details regarding the altercation, I think it's safe to assume that the offense went beyond the use of the word itself. Sometimes, in the heat of anger, we can appear more threatening or menacing than we realize. I'd focus less on the word and more on the situation itself—especially the lack of control that caused it. Regardless, the safest path forward is not to use profanity, because you can never determine if such language will have a negative impact and lead to repercussions."

"Understood," said Brown, somewhat sheepishly. "Good advice." He started to stand but paused. "Please know I'm not trying to make excuses for myself. I'm just trying to understand."

Dara nodded and smiled kindly as Andrew thanked her for her time. He told her that he had contacted Ginnie Parvich and had an appointment to see her the next day. He assured Dara that he was taking this ordeal seriously and hoped to turn a bad, embarrassing situation into an opportunity for positive growth. He told her that he would keep her informed of his progress.

Dara Klein nodded. "My door is always open."

The Department of Psychiatry and Institute at the University of New York was world renowned. Established in 1895, the institute was one of the first programs in the United States to integrate teaching, research, and therapeutic approaches to the care of patients with mental illnesses. Today, it is not only one of the largest departments in the country in terms of faculty size and research, but it is also among the top-ranked psychiatry programs in the nation, a place where Nobel laureates perform investigations on the function of the human brain.

Ginnie Parvich was the director of clinical psychology, and her specialty was behavior modification. Her office in the City of New York Psychiatric Hospital Outpatient Building was connected to the main hospital via a pedestrian bridge across Harbor Avenue. As Andrew walked to his first session, he paused on the bridge for a moment's reflection, taking in the city's skyline. He had seen it hundreds, thousands, maybe even tens of thousands of times, but it never ceased to amaze him. Its scope and grandeur were a testament to industry—a triumph of human accomplishment. Within it pulsed the beating heart of a city whose vitality and energy were unparalleled. It could make or break, elevate or destroy. He took a deep breath to steady himself and continued his walk to the psych building. Exiting the elevator on the ninth floor, he took a seat and waited patiently until called to see the doctor.

Ginnie Parvich, a middle-aged, smartly dressed woman in a light brown suit and beige blouse, had been at the Psych Institute her entire 20-year career. She extended her hand to Andrew and asked him to join her in her office, where the two doctors made polite introductions, agreeing to call one another by first names.

Ginnie sat at her desk, while Andrew sat on a small loveseat facing her. Ginnie's office was comfortable, with diplomas and a poster of Van Gogh's

The Starry Night from the MOMA gift shop affixed to the wall behind her desk. Ginnie told Andrew that any notes she took would remain confidential, and assured him that their conversations would not be available in EPIC, the medical center's computerized record system.

"Start at the beginning," she prompted.

Andrew told her about the monthlong administrative timeout imposed by the hospital to investigate the charges levied by a hospital employee. The situation had been, and continued to be, humiliating—an embarrassment that had dragged on too long, primarily due to human resources and nursing investigators being on vacation.

"I dangled in the wind while people were sunbathing at the beach," he said, expressing his anger freely for the first time outside of conversations with his family. "Frankly, I was pissed off, but I had no recourse."

He continued, uninterrupted for several minutes, admitting that the allegations were true. He had lost his temper, cursed, pounded on the desk. He explained the circumstances surrounding the outburst, but acknowledged that they were no excuse.

"I was rightfully enraged," he said. "But, given my rank and position, I acted inappropriately."

Ginnie Parvich sat stoically throughout his monologue, nodding slowly but otherwise betraying little emotion. When he finished, she allowed what he had said to sit between them. The minute's silence felt an eternity to the still seething Andrew Brown.

"Andrew," she said, finally, "it is clear to me that this has been an emotionally trying ordeal, and I can certainly understand your frustration. I would like very much to work with you, and I think that I can be of some help." She paused. "But I wonder if you are ready to accept that help and put in the work that is necessary for change."

Andrew started to speak, but Ginnie continued.

"I believe that you understand the gravity of your situation, but I wonder if you are able to appreciate the true depth of your own complicity." She spoke in a kind, soft voice as she continued. "I want you to feel safe and comfortable here. I want you to express yourself openly and honestly. But it is also my job to hold you to account—not to coddle you. I want to push you to truly understand the *root* of your anger so that you can get a handle on it and control it. For your job, yes, but more importantly for your relationships with your family and yourself. Does that sound like what *you* want from this as well?"

Andrew was taken aback.

"*Of course,* I want that," he said haltingly, through tense jaws.

Inwardly, he noted in surprise that the irritation bubbling in his chest was not anger. He thought to himself, *not even close.*

He began again, his voice stilted. "I'm here of my own accord, Ginnie. This wasn't a requirement, but I recognize the problem and I want to fix it." Had she not heard him? Understood his experience, the unfairness of this ordeal?

"I understand that," Ginnie replied evenly, as if she had read his thoughts. "And I respect it. I want to help you. But to do this work, you will have to confront some of your own worst impulses, head on. Some of your most painful and embarrassing memories. I assume that this is not the first time your anger has gotten out of control?"

Andrew drew in a deep breath. Like she said, honesty was required for this to work. Honesty with Ginnie—and with himself. "There have been times I've lost my temper. But it's certainly the first time it's come to *this*," he said, his heart rate again accelerating as he recalled the purpose of his visit. He looked across the table at Ginnie, her gaze leveling. He felt safe with her. He respected her accolades, of course—otherwise he would never have made the appointment—but upon meeting her in person, he found that he felt, perhaps for the first time in his life, that he could be truly honest with someone other than his wife.

"But yes, there have been other incidents." He thought of that summer at Serge's camp, of that time in the driveway with Marissa's parents, of countless evenings…

"I want to do this," he said. "I do."

"Good. So do I." Ginnie looked at her watch. "Our time is up for today, but I have homework for you. I want you to delve into your past and recall when, where, and how situations have evolved into anger. I want to know the inciting events and your responses—everything, every detail. I understand that this will be painful, but please be as clinical as possible. We'll work through these together in our next session."

Andrew nodded, blinking. That was it, time to go. He rose from his seat, dozens of unspoken sentences lodged in his throat.

"Thank you, Ginnie," he said.

* * *

After a quiet dinner that evening, Andrew and Marissa retired to the sunroom of their Dobbs Ferry apartment, opening the sliding glass balcony doors to allow the sounds of the city to float in on the cool evening breeze. Andrew had left his initial session with Ginnie feeling somehow both invigorated and cowed. On his drive home, he had rehashed the conversation with Ginnie repeatedly, mulling over what she had said, what he hadn't said, repleading his case. As much as he tried to avoid it, he knew in his gut that she was right—this went beyond the "fuck" incident to something deeper, something within his very being that terrified him.

Am I even capable of change? Andrew wondered. As far back as he could remember, he'd treated anger as a sort of currency. It was his father's preferred method for asserting dominance in his childhood home, and one that Andrew had subconsciously mimicked in adulthood. It bore results, sure, though there were casualties...

"So, how did it go?" Marissa asked, jumping in headfirst. She was nervous but steadfast. She knew her husband.

"Well," he said, taking a sip of the La Croix he often drank in lieu of alcohol. "I trust her." He paused for a moment, gazing again at the skyline. In so many ways it represented everything that he had built, everything that he had worked so hard for.

"I trust that she can help me," he said before adding, "and I know that I need help. I'm sorry I've been such a nightmare this past month." He paused, pressing his lips together. "I'm sorry that I've been such a nightmare, period."

He took her hand in his and stroked it gently with his thumb. "But I want to change. I *have* to change. I know that I fucked up—that I've fucked up so many times," he was talking fast now, his words tumbling over one another as tears welled in his eyes. "I've fucked up with you, with our kids. I need to be better. For Pia, for the grandkids. I just—I want to be better for them. The job—the job can go to hell, but—"

"I love you," Marissa said with a strength that left Andrew breathless. She clasped her husband's hand tightly in her own, remembering the call from Serge's camp, huddling with the children inside the house, the doors locked, her parents' taillights pulling down the driveway. She remembered, in vivid detail, every tense evening of the past month, bundling herself away to meet her husband's needs, his mercurial moods.

"I love you, and I'm proud of you. So *fucking* proud of you." She smiled at him, and holding onto each other tightly, they laughed for the first time in a month.

CHAPTER 4

MEMORIES OF ANGER PAST

Precise dates might be difficult to recall, but the incidents themselves were deeply imprinted in Andrew's cerebral cortex. He decided to select two examples—one specific, one general and much more common. He sat down at his desk and took notes so as to capture every painful, granular detail. He wanted to leave no stone unturned. Ginnie's homework was not going to be easy.

Taking a deep, steadying breath, Andrew let the memory of the first incident wash over him. Decades ago, at their home in Tenafly, the red and gold autumn leaves seemed to blaze in the late afternoon sun. It was an early Sunday evening in November, and the family had planned a dinner with Marissa's parents, Peter and Janet, at Arturo's Italian in the neighboring town of Haworth.

The kids, just eight and five years old at the time, sauntered merrily out of the house in light, unzipped jackets. The evening was cool, and the temperature would only continue to fall.

Andrew told them to button up before getting into the car for the short ride to the restaurant.

They ignored him.

"Zip your jackets," he repeated.

No response.

"*Goddammit close your jackets, or you're not coming!*" he growled.

The temper had metastasized and burst forth before he even recognized it forming.

Startled by the sudden turn in their father's tone, the children stopped in their tracks.

"Leave them alone, Andrew," Marissa said with a sigh, coming, as she often did, to her children's defense. "Get in the car, kids."

Andrew, ignoring Marissa's attempts at placation, raised his voice still higher. "Do as I tell you, and button your jackets! *Now!*"

The children looked to Marissa for guidance, and again, she told them to get into the car. "Pia, sit on Grandpa's lap. Serge, you sit with me in the front."

The veins in Andrew's temples throbbed as his blood pressure and anger mounted. In only a matter of moments, he had already found himself beyond the point of no return.

As the kids climbed silently into the car, he thundered, "These fucking kids have to learn to listen to me, Marissa, and you're not helping by fucking *coddling them!*" He slammed his fist on the hood of the blue Volvo. The sudden physical expression of anger and adrenaline felt like a valve releasing from a pressure cooker. He punched the car three times, four times, his knuckles bruising on impact with the freezing metal of the hood as he chased the release of his fury.

The children cowered open-mouthed, fearful their father would hit them—Janet and Peter were dumbfounded, speechless. Marissa stood her ground, her demeanor calm, which only further infuriated Andrew.

Jerking open the car door, he said, "Pia—Serge—get out of the car. We're not going. Out of the car—now!" He attempted to pull Pia out onto the driveway.

That was too much. "Don't you *dare* touch those kids!" Marissa warned.

Andrew whirled, sticking a menacing finger in her face. "Don't tell me what to do. Who do you think you are? Out of my way!"

Marissa, no stranger to Andrew's violent temper, tried desperately to de-escalate the situation. She told the kids to get out of the car and wait in the garden. With a pang, she noticed that Pia and Serge had zipped up their jackets as far as they'd go.

Peter and Janet also got out of the car, leaving the doors open. Peter asked Marissa if she was all right, and she assured her father that she could handle the situation. Nervously, they told Marissa that they were leaving, and said goodbye to the grandchildren. Janet told Marissa that she would call her later that evening. They didn't say a word to Andrew. They didn't even look at him as they got into their SUV and drove away.

If the presence of Marissa's parents had tempered Andrew, however slightly, their departure had the opposite effect. He directed his rage at the open car doors, which he slammed shut. Without a word, Marissa gathered the kids, hurried them inside the house, and locked the door firmly behind her.

"Open the *fucking* door, *bitch!*"

He ran around to the front door, only to find that it was locked as well. He'd left his keys inside. Marissa and the kids were safe.

Andrew, alone with his rage, sat on the stone wall separating the driveway from the lawn and garden, feeling his anger ebb more and more with each passing second. Before long, his anger had dissipated entirely, replaced by shame. The storm of fury that had struck him so suddenly had disappeared just as quickly, but the damage was done. Thankfully, he had caused no physical harm—Marissa, Pia, and Serge were unscathed, physically at least—but he no longer recognized himself.

* * *

Andrew sat back in his chair, blinking at his laptop. The incident had happened decades ago, but he remembered each detail as if it'd been merely hours. His gut twisted.

That he would have to recount these details next week to Dr. Parvich felt unbearable. How could he look her in the eye and tell her that he had called his wife a bitch—that he had tried to forcefully pull his tiny daughter out of the car.

Andrew's shoulders slumped, and he wondered whether he was truly prepared for the task ahead of him. He was choosing to take on this journey, and he could just as easily choose not to. But he knew, in his heart, that it wasn't really a choice—not if he wanted to live with integrity. He wanted desperately, more than anything, to be a safe, supportive grandfather to Pia's children. There had never been any question of his deep and unflinching love for his family, but he knew that he had made mistakes, countless mistakes, with his own children. He refused to take the easy way out.

* * *

The next evening, after a gorgeous dinner of roast chicken and fennel, carefully prepared by Marissa, Andrew settled back into his work. The second incident was, in some ways, more painful to recall than the first, since it had involved so many people outside of his own family.

Thirty years ago, Serge had attended Camp Echo Sky in Honesdale, Pennsylvania, along the Delaware Water Gap. The camp owner, Mitchell Press, asked Andrew if he would consider being the camp doctor for the first two weeks of the season. The camp of 300 boys had a reputation for emphasizing athletics and needed pediatricians to staff the infirmary in two-week blocks. As compensation, the doctor's son attended camp for free. Andrew enjoyed sports—tennis, golf, basketball, swimming—and he knew Serge did too, so he figured, why not?

The first day of camp, a Saturday morning, Marissa drove Serge to the bus pickup location in the Cross-County Shopping Center parking lot in Yonkers. Andrew, alone, left earlier and drove himself, wanting to meet the camp nurses and assist in setting up the infirmary before the campers arrived. He would have driven Serge himself, but they both wanted him to get the full camp experience with the other kids.

The doctor had a private bungalow adjacent to the infirmary, with a king-size bed covered with yellow-stained linens and a severely faded blue blanket. The rest of the room was sparsely furnished with two uncomfortable chairs, a small wooden dresser upon which sat a 12-inch black and white TV, and an old air conditioner in the window that rattled and spewed dust and mildew. The accommodations were less than luxurious, but it was summer camp, after all. Andrew decided he could make it work, or at least try his best.

The buses arrived at midafternoon, unloading hundreds of boys of all shapes and sizes, aged 8 to 18, and dressed in the camp uniform of blue shorts and white T-shirts emblazoned with the Camp Echo Sky logo of a soaring eagle. Mitchell Press and his assistant, Don Casey, greeted everyone at the flagpole to raise the American flag and recite the Pledge of Allegiance. Don gave the assembled multitude their marching orders for the remainder of the day. He dismissed the campers and counselors with instructions to go to their bunks, unpack, make up the bunks, and write a postcard home to tell their parents that they had arrived safely.

Scheduled infirmary hours were three times per day, after each meal. The most common complaints were stomach aches from a change in the drinking water, and homesickness. Treatment mostly consisted of Tylenol and soothing conversation. Serge settled in easily. He seemed to like his bunkmates and enjoyed his activities of roller hockey, soccer, and swimming. Andrew played tennis every day with one of the instructors, one-on-one basketball against Mitch Press—a very competitive guy—and read *The*

Firm by John Grisham and *Chutzpah* by Alan Dershowitz. Marissa joined Andrew the second week. She was in antique heaven and in the evening, they went to the movies in Port Jervis. As enjoyable as it was, Andrew's time at Echo Sky was not a vacation—he was constantly busy with the campers. Thankfully, nothing too serious ever occurred, but he had his hands full nonetheless. Of greatest value to Andrew, Serge was able to attend camp at no cost, a huge savings for a great opportunity.

Mitchell asked Andrew to return to camp the next summer with the same deal, and Andrew readily agreed.

The following summer, the buses arrived, and the routine was identical to the previous year—but there was a hitch. Serge had requested a specific bunk to be with his friends, but Don Casey had assigned him to another lodge with all new kids.

Serge was devastated. He had waited all school year to see his friends. "This sucks!" he opined. "It's not fair! I'm not staying!"

Andrew spoke with Casey, but he was told that there was nothing to be done. There had been too many requests for the same bunk, and when the time came to make the decision, they had thought Serge would be mature enough to handle it. Casey spun it as a compliment, but Serge wouldn't hear it. Andrew tried to reason with his son, but he would not budge.

"I'm leaving. I *hate* camp!" Serge began to cry—his summer was ruined.

Andrew could feel his patience wearing thin as he continued to try to sway his son. Serge refused to unpack his trunk or make his bunk. He threw a tantrum and ran away. Andrew, exhausted from a long day of travel and set up and humiliated by his son's behavior, lost it. He chased Serge, yelling and making a scene.

"*You little shit, who do you think you are?* Get back here, and get your ass into the bunk!" In his rage, Andrew knocked over garbage cans and threw the covers at his son. His profanity intensified—his temper was completely out of control. He hadn't even noticed the crowd that had gathered around him until Don Casey and Mitchell were physically restraining him.

"Calm down, please calm down!" they urged. "Go to the office, Dr. Brown. *Now*."

It was one of the lowest points in Andrew's adult life. Once the anger had receded, he felt lower than low. So low that he had to look up to look down. Not only had he raged against his son, but he had done so in public. Three hundred campers, counselors, and staff members had witnessed his horrific display. He was humiliated. And beyond his own repercussions, there was Serge's anger, fear, and embarrassment. How could he face his friends and fellow campers after they'd seen his father act so egregiously?

His son was only nine years old and ill-equipped to understand the events of the day. All he knew was that one minute, he was railing against a personal injustice and the next moment, his father, whom he respected highly, was even more out of control than he was. A family pattern, perhaps, though one that was much more understandable in a nine-year-old. Serge was more than upset with his father, more than disappointed. An apology and request for forgiveness would not cut it—not today.

Sheepishly and with great pain, Andrew called Marissa and recounted what had transpired. She was speechless. She did not berate her husband—what could be gained from it? She urged him to stay calm and focus on Serge. She reminded him that their son was his only priority. Despite her subdued tone, Andrew couldn't help imagining what she must think of him. He could feel her secondhand embarrassment, the blame that she would inevitably shoulder, her fear for her child's safety. She knew her husband, and she loved him deeply, but she was fiercely protective of her children and if it ever came down to it, she would sacrifice anything to protect them, even her relationship with Andrew. They weren't at that point yet, and Andrew hoped to God they never would be, but this incident put them at least another step closer.

Mitchell and Don recognized that their priority, first and foremost, was the safety of the campers whose parents had entrusted their well-being for the summer to Camp Echo Sky. They spoke with Serge privately and suggested he spend the night in Mitchell's private home on the camp grounds. In the morning, they would reassign him to his friends' bunkhouse.

Mitchell told Andrew that, under the circumstances, he could not stay at the camp. Mitchell had already spoken to a family medicine doctor at the Port Jervis Regional Hospital, and he had consented to be available for the thrice-daily infirmary hours until a replacement could be found.

Andrew's embarrassment was compounded. The idea that the camp had already taken steps to call in a replacement somehow added to his humiliation—that another doctor within his network would hear, firsthand, about his outburst was unimaginable. He was despondent. He apologized profusely and pleaded for forgiveness, asking Mitchell if he would consider allowing him to fulfill his obligation and return later in the summer.

The Camp Echo Sky owner pursed his lips noncommittally. "Andrew, you are my friend. I care for your family, and I am truly fond of Serge, but I need time to think, rearrange schedules, and determine what is best for everyone. I need some time. I will get back to you in a couple days."

"If possible, Mitchell, I would like to return."

Mitchell called Andrew the next day. "Serge seems fine. He's happy in his new bunk with his friends. I discussed your return with Don and, most importantly, with your son, who is having a great time. We agreed that you can come back to camp the last two weeks of the season, August 2nd through the 15th, with one caveat: Marissa must accompany you for the entire tenure, the full two weeks."

Mitchell recognized that Marissa was Andrew's rudder.

"Agreed. Thank you."

The weeks leading up to Andrew's return to Camp Echo Sky were difficult. He was moody and needy, and while Marissa did her best to keep him grounded, there was only so much she could endure. She was angry at her husband for his outburst and heartbroken for Serge, but she knew that she had to stay strong if they were to get through the end of the summer unscathed. She needed, more than anything, for Andrew's makeup weeks at Camp Echo Sky to go smoothly, for him to reconcile with Serge and make amends for his past actions.

The last two weeks of the camp season were always the most exciting, filled with special events and intercamp games and banquets, all culminating in "color war"—a three-day competition that divided the camp in half, pitting the white team against the blue. By the time Andrew and Marissa arrived, the campers were up to their eyeballs in activities and weepily anticipating summer's end. They went virtually unnoticed, and even Serge, consumed with his friends and activities, paid them little attention. Andrew was relieved. He knew that this would not make up for his previous behavior—not by a long shot—but it was a good sign, nonetheless.

Throughout the remaining weeks, Andrew remained on his best behavior. There was little to do in the infirmary—no serious physical incidents occurred, and homesickness tended to dissipate toward the end of summer. Having Marissa there was also steadying. The blue team won the color wars, and the season ended uneventfully.

CHAPTER 5

THE PATH TO CHANGE

Wednesday's meeting with Ginnie could not come soon enough. Recounting those past incidents had been painful—excruciating, really. Time may heal plenty, but Andrew knew that he would never forget the look of shame in Serge's eyes when he knocked over the garbage can, or the horror on Marissa's parents' faces as they pulled out of the driveway, refusing to look at him.

Of course, he had not embarked on this painful exercise for nothing. He knew that this step was critical if he ever hoped to make substantial changes. But he was nevertheless anxious to share his past foibles with Ginnie Parvich. It was too much for him to hold alone. As he walked across the pedestrian bridge, the details of the incidents played through his mind, a never-ending loop of his most shameful moments. In his arms, he held a folder filled with notes, but they were hardly necessary. The egregious confrontations may have occurred 30 years prior, but they may as well have happened yesterday. Andrew was certain that Marissa, Pia, and Serge remembered them as clearly as he did…he wished that was not the case.

"Hi, Andrew. How are you today?" Rather than sit behind her desk, Dr. Parvich sat in a chair opposite Andrew, notepad at the ready on her lap. She hoped to make the session feel intimate and welcoming, allowing Andrew to feel more comfortable as he revealed these most painful and private memories.

"I'm well, Ginnie. And you?" He breathed steadily, his heart pounding in anticipation.

"Are you ready?"

"As ready as I could ever be, I guess."

The exercise was not comfortable. He'd much prefer not having to revisit the skeletons in his closet, but the situation required it, and he'd made a promise to his wife and colleagues. And there was a part of him that yearned to discuss these painful memories, to get them off his chest after so many years and hand them to someone else.

"I see you took notes and wrote things down, as I recommended," Ginnie said, nodding appreciatively. "Feel free to use them if that would be helpful. If you don't mind, I'd like to keep them for future reference."

"Well," he muttered. "Here goes." Taking a deep breath, he dove in.

Andrew told Ginnie about the incident with the children and their jackets. He admitted that, in retrospect, his demands for obedience from Pia and Serge were unreasonable. The likelihood of any harm befalling the children because of their open jackets was remote. He recognized, as he recounted the incident, that it had nothing to do with the jackets—it was about control, plain and simple. As their father, Andrew demanded respect and obedience from Pia and Serge—they should not defy him but do as they were told.

Ginnie asked Andrew if he thought his response was appropriate, given the circumstances.

He replied that, obviously, it was not.

She asked him how he felt about his wife defending the children rather than supporting him from the beginning.

Thinking for a moment, Andrew replied, "It was instinctive." She was protecting her offspring from attack by a rabid dog, he explained. Her maternal instincts prevailed over all else—protect the young at all costs. Words were harmful, profanity unacceptable, but bodily hurt to the kids was another thing entirely. She would not, could not, permit that to happen.

Ginnie sat silent for a moment, considering Andrew. "How did you feel when Marissa shielded the children?" Her tone was not unkind. "Do you think she should have told the kids to close their jackets? Could that have ended the anger and outburst?"

Contemplating his answer, Andrew rubbed his chin, "Honestly, it's hard to say. I guess she didn't see it as necessary to agree with me."

"But how did *you* see it?"

"Well, in general…in general, I believe it's important for parents to be on the same page, delivering a consistent message. Partially, I was pissed because I wanted Marissa to embrace that message from the beginning, from the moment I told the kids to zip their jackets and before I spiraled out of control. But I was already irritated, and knowing Marissa…well, she knows me. I'm sure she knew where it was going—where it was going to go regardless…So, it wasn't a situation about parenting styles—that was clear almost immediately."

Ginnie nodded, jotting a note on her pad before leveling her gaze at Andrew. "So, even if Marissa had immediately agreed with you and told the kids to zip up their jackets, even then, the situation probably would have ended as it had?"

"Almost certainly," he replied. He had gone from zero to 60 in a heartbeat, falling into a violent maelstrom of anger in an instant. It mattered little how his wife responded, agreeing with him or instinctively protecting the children. But Marissa's actions were correct.

"So what finally defused the situation?"

He explained that his in-laws had driven off—wanting no part of his abhorrent behavior—and that Marissa and the children had escaped to the safety of the house, locking the doors behind him. He had been left alone on the driveway with no one left to rail against. He had sat on the garden wall, closed his eyes, took a deep breath—several actually—and the rage slowly dissipated. "It took a long time, though," he added, ashamed.

The doctor asked Andrew to think about what he had just said. She repeated, "You sat on the wall, closed your eyes, and breathed deeply. *You sat on the wall, closed your eyes, and breathed deeply.* What do think might have happened if, rather than attack your children, you had sat on the wall, closed your eyes, and taken deep breaths in the first place?"

Andrew sat thinking silently.

She suggested that they put this thought in the proverbial parking lot for the moment. "We'll come back to it later. Tell me about the next incident you reflected on."

As Andrew recalled the episode at Camp Echo Sky, Ginnie's expression changed—it was obvious she was uncomfortable. Andrew felt self-conscious and pleaded with her not to judge or think less of him—he felt humiliated. Despite the fact that the event had occurred 30 years ago, the details were forever ingrained on his conscience.

Dr. Parvich assured him that her purpose was to help provide him with tools to control and mitigate his anger—she was not there to judge him. She did, however, admit that she found the incident difficult to comprehend.

"Where do you think the anger came from?" she asked, her voice younger than he'd yet heard.

His voice was heavy with years of regret as he said, "I wish I knew."

He told the doctor this was one of the lowest—if not the single worst—incidents of his life. He could not recall a specific trigger. Remembering the incident, he was baffled. He couldn't understand how he could have behaved so badly.

That day's events had not only affected him but had a long-lasting negative impact on Serge. It had strained the relationship he shared with his son for years—perhaps even to this day. He reasoned, in retrospect, that his response should have been to advocate for Serge rather than to denounce him. A calm, private conversation with the owner and head counselor of the camp would have hopefully secured Serge the bunk he wanted, or at the very least might have helped Andrew gain a better understanding of their decision, which he could have subsequently relayed to his son.

Sometimes life wasn't fair—every kid had to learn that lesson—but Andrew's own response had been beyond unfair. He had directed the totality of his rage at his defenseless nine-year-old son. Because he was throwing and kicking garbage cans, someone might really have been injured. It was a selfish, narcissistic, despicable performance.

Holding nothing back, he told the doctor the display of anger had occurred in front of hundreds of campers, counselors, staff, and the infirmary nurses. Terrible, just terrible. Horrible for him, horrible for Serge, humiliating for him, humiliating for Serge…Inexcusable.

Dr. Parvich asked Brown what he thought would have happened if he had sat on the proverbial wall, closed his eyes, and taken deep breaths.

"I couldn't," he replied, shaking his head. "Not in that moment. It all happened way too quickly."

"Perhaps it felt impossible then," said Ginnie, "but that's because you hadn't practiced. You didn't know to look for the warning signs, or how to catch yourself before the ball started rolling down the hill."

She told Andrew that he already possessed some of the essential tools needed to avert violent anger, and that together they would strategize how to effectively use behavioral mitigation instruments to help him control his outbursts.

Ginnie thanked Andrew for his candor and willingness to share such painful memories.

"Let's switch gears here. You said earlier that the incident at camp had a lasting negative impact on your relationship with your son. Can you tell me more about that?"

Andrew told Ginnie that, following his outburst, Serge was distant, not very communicative, and perhaps resentful. It was hard for Andrew to know for certain whether his attitude was directly related to the camp incident, but it was clear that they were not as close as they'd once been. It was not for lack of trying, though. He and Serge spent time together every weekend on the road, traveling to hockey games and tournaments from New England to Maryland, but their conversations were strained and did not flow easily.

"To be honest, Ginnie, I was envious of some of the other dads. I did my best, but something was missing. Serge was close to his mother, thank goodness for that. Marissa was incredible with him."

"What was Serge like as a teenager? Did things improve?" Ginnie asked.

"Well, no, things weren't much better. I tried to introduce Serge to golf, but he had no interest. I suggested we go to some New Jersey Devils hockey games or Yankees games—no interest. Fishing—no interest. We just didn't spend much time together."

In high school, Serge, for the most part, stayed out of trouble. He smoked marijuana, but nothing beyond weed. Fortunately, he ran with a good crowd, and his friends were good students who aspired to attend top-rated colleges. Serge went to Columbia, but even though he was only 10 miles from home, Andrew rarely heard from him. He might as well have been in California or on another planet.

"Don't ask me how, but he graduated with honors and a degree in film studies," Andrew said with a grin.

Serge was extraordinarily knowledgeable about film and its history and aspired to be a filmmaker. He actually had some talent but was ill-prepared to make it on his own after college. He refused to take any advice from his parents and refused to go to graduate school at Tisch, NYU's film school, to enhance his craft. He professed that a writer should write, an artist should create art, and a filmmaker should make films—school was unnecessary for creativity.

"He did, reluctantly, allow me to support him financially for some time after college. It was my pleasure, actually. Marissa and I decided it was worth the monthly stipend to have him live with his buddies rather than back in our home, which would have been a mistake for sure." Andrew's face fell. "However, rather than ease tensions, the money created more resentment and drove us further apart."

As time passed, Serge began to enjoy some professional success. He made music videos and commercials for Chase Bank, Nabisco, and others, as well as two or three short films and a children's television series.

"I no longer had to support him financially, which was a really good development for both of us. Building a career helped Serge feel better about himself and also to appreciate what I did professionally as a physician. Over the past few years, we've begun to talk more. He asks my opinion about a variety of subjects. We discuss climate change, politics, and our common disdain for Trump.

"One day, recently, I told Serge that I loved him and he replied, 'Dad, I love you too.'" Andrew smiled fondly.

"Thank you for sharing all of that, Andrew," Ginnie said. "It sounds like a combination of factors have helped you two find common ground. The passage of time can help heal old wounds, and, of course, Serge finding his own professional and financial footing must have helped him feel like he could meet you on more even ground. Have you told him about the work that we're doing together—that you're making this effort to reform your behavior?"

He sighed. "I haven't. Not yet. Maybe Marissa has, but if she has, she didn't tell me."

"Well, he might be happy to hear that you're putting in this work." Ginnie looked at her watch. "We're out of time, but I do have another assignment for next week."

Andrew groaned, and they both laughed.

"I want you to think about your relationship with your wife and examine what causes discord. What are the triggers that set you off? I'd like to discuss Marissa's reactions to your outbursts, and the ways in which her behavior and your tendencies within your relationship may be helping or hindering these cycles of rage."

Andrew nodded and stood to shake the doctor's hand.

"I know this was a difficult session, Andrew. Change is uncomfortable—painful sometimes—but without hard work, you will not see any rewards."

Andrew turned to leave but stopped short at her door. "Do you believe that anger can be inherited?"

"Interesting question," Ginnie said. "Let's discuss that next week."

CHAPTER 6

ANDREW AND MARISSA

Andrew was spent. It was a balmy day in early fall and rather than take the pedestrian bridge back to his office in the Powell Building, he decided to walk outside. He stopped at Starbucks for a flat white and sat down to drink it on a bench in the garden. He closed his eyes and, for a few minutes, did nothing but breathe. Once he had finished his coffee, he checked the calendar on his phone and, seeing that he had nothing scheduled for the remainder of the day, decided to call it quits. He stopped at his office to check his emails one last time, then gathered his papers and told his assistant that he was leaving for the day.

Marissa was in the kitchen of their Dobbs Ferry apartment when Andrew arrived home. It was her favorite room, and reading recipes, cooking, and baking was a true passion. She loved the entire process, from planning the menu to shopping at specialty markets and preparing and presenting the food. Her skills were incredible. She had no weaknesses, from hors d'oeuvres to ricotta cheesecake—everything she created was always beyond delectable.

Marissa looked up from a recipe card. "Hi, honey. How was your day?"

Andrew told her things were all right, uneventful, but that the session with the psychologist had been an unwelcome reminder of incidents he'd rather forget. He told her he felt simultaneously terrible and relieved. "I mean, my God," he said, "I can really be an awful person."

Marissa was sympathetic but firm. "You aren't an awful person, Andrew. You've just done some awful things. Patterns are hard to break, and you've been in this pattern of anger since I met you. It will take a lot of work to change."

"I just hope I can," Andrew said heavily.

Marissa crossed the kitchen to take his hands in hers. "Of course, you can."

Andrew smiled, comforted. "Do you mind if we go out tonight? O'Mandarin in Hartsdale? I need an egg roll."

"Sure. Take out the dog—I just fed her—and I'll get ready."

O'Mandarin was popular and always crowded with patrons waiting to be seated. After about 10 minutes, Andrew and Marissa were seated in a booth along the far wall. They were familiar with the menu, and when the server approached, they were ready with their order: soup dumplings, honey boneless ribs, basil chicken, shredded orange beef, dried sautéed string beans, and the Chengdu house special fried rice.

It was far too much food, but they would eat the leftovers for lunch or dinner the next day, as was their standard practice. Looking across the table at his wife, Andrew thought about how grateful he was for their routines— for all the many mundane trivialities that they shared—that grounded them in their relationship, their family, and their individual lives. Reliving those incidents from the past, he felt painfully aware of how quickly any of this might have been taken away from him, how easy it would have been for Marissa to take the kids and go to her parents, who would have surely understood after witnessing his display in the driveway.

Dinner passed quickly and pleasantly. Andrew did not repeat the details from his session with Dr. Parvich. Their time together during meals was sacred ground, and they did their best to avoid heavy topics or upheaval of any sort. Instead, the conversation revolved around their children and plans for the weekend. Still, in the back of his mind, Andrew considered his homework. Pleasant as dinner was, it wouldn't be difficult to pinpoint the inciting incidents of anger between him and his wife—there were plenty. But that was a task for tomorrow. At the end of the evening, they waddled with full bellies to the car, laden with crackling takeout containers, and headed home.

* * *

Ginnie Parvich felt the need to decompress that evening as well. She lived in a spacious eight-room apartment on West End Avenue with her husband Lawrence Shine, an interventional cardiologist at the University of New York Hospital, and their five-year-old daughter, Maya.

Ginnie, appropriately, rarely spoke about her patients with Lawrence, but the evening after she had seen Andrew Brown, she could not restrain herself. She did not go into details about the content or reason for his visit, only that he was a new patient. She asked her husband if he knew Brown, and he told her he knew who Andrew was but did not know him personally. Lawrence opened his laptop and searched for Brown on the university's faculty website.

"Wow! Well, he's definitely no slouch," he said, scrolling through Brown's accolades. "He's had an endowed university professorship and has been the director of pediatric oncology. He was nationally recognized for his clinical investigation in lymphoma…He's currently a vice chair of pediatrics, *and* he founded a charity that raised millions of dollars for children with cancer. Does this guy even sleep?"

Ginnie wondered to herself how someone with such a violent temper could be so successful. There must be a disconnect…

Pondering Andrew's question regarding the hereditary nature of anger, she contemplated whether professionals with temper issues could channel their outrage into something positive. Although she was an expert in behavior modification, her knowledge about anger was limited. She decided to suggest to Andrew that they educate themselves about the history and genetic aspects of anger. It would be an opportunity for her to gain Andrew's trust, to demonstrate to him that she respected his intelligence and saw him as capable of taking an active role in his own treatment. Surely someone with his success would appreciate that.

* * *

Over the course of the week, in anticipation of his upcoming session with Ginnie, Andrew dedicated himself to his homework. This week's task of identifying the triggers within his relationship proved easier and less traumatizing than the previous week's. Marissa had several habits that consistently pressed his buttons. These behaviors, which might seem trivial to outsiders, were a constant irritant to Andrew. Marissa was always late, whereas he would describe himself as punctual, a Japanese bullet train, always on schedule.

Marissa's lack of punctuality irritated Andrew because, on a fundamental level, he found it disrespectful—of his time and whomever else's they were set to meet. Being on time took some extra planning and effort, but nothing herculean. Yet, no matter how many times he had made it clear to his wife that he was bothered by her tardiness, it persisted.

Marissa's lateness often sparked Andrew's anger past the point of irritation, and he responded by raising his voice, using profanity, and slamming his fist. While he had never resorted to physical violence, his rage spiraled out of control, concluding only when they had reached their destination. When he was growing up, Andrew's mother had always been late as well. It had been a constant source of irritation to his father and often triggered his temper. And Andrew was his father's son.

Another trigger for Andrew was breaking his diet. He wasn't terribly overweight, but his vanity required that he keep constant vigilance over his intake. Unfortunately, maintaining a restrictive diet was challenging, and Andrew frequently blamed others—Marissa in particular—for his missteps, telling her that it was her fault that he'd eaten four cookies instead of one, too large a portion of pasta, or too many slices of pizza. He was unable to accept responsibility for his own actions, and it was easier to blame his wife. He begged her not to bake chocolate chip cookies, or buy candy and ice cream, and to serve smaller portions. He reasoned if the stuff weren't in the house, he couldn't eat it. Of course, it was her house too, and she argued that she should be allowed to snack as she wished—why should she be held to Andrew's diet?

Still, it infuriated Andrew, and when Marissa disobeyed him, Andrew would boil over with anger, slamming his fist on the kitchen counter and railing against his wife for no rational reason. It was far easier to blame her for his failure. This behavior was ongoing and frequent.

Thinking about this latter issue, Andrew felt embarrassed. At least his irritation over Marissa's lateness was understandable—no one liked to be kept waiting. But his childish inability to practice self-restraint and even more childish practice of blaming his wife for his own lack of self-control was, well, embarrassing.

Still, he was eager to discuss these thoughts with Ginnie. Patterns were beginning to emerge, mostly surrounding his desire to be in control, but also pertaining to his childhood. Thinking back to his last session, he vowed to return to the question he had asked Ginnie on his way out. Could anger be inherited?

* * *

The following Wednesday, Andrew greeted Ginnie's receptionist and paid his copay.

"She's ready for you, go right in."

Ginnie sat directly across from him with a notepad on her lap. Andrew told her that during the past week he had been thinking nonstop about anger, its origins, its diagnosis, and management...And, of course, its origins within his marriage.

"Let's start there," Ginnie said. "How did you and your wife meet? Give me some background, and then let's dig a little deeper into the issues you've identified as triggers."

Andrew told Dr. Parvich that his sister Margaret had known Marissa and had suggested that he call and ask her out. Their first date had been one for the books. It was Andrew's 30th birthday, and they'd had drinks at the famous Blue Bar at the Algonquin Hotel, three blocks from Marissa's office in the jewelry district. Marissa worked in a family jewelry design and manufacturing company, J & N Sage, alongside her two sisters. Although small, the company was famous for its beautiful and contemporary designs. They had won a Coty Award, were in the DeBeers Diamond Hall of Fame, and were vendors to the best stores—Neiman Marcus, Saks, and Bloomingdale's.

Marissa ran the business side of the company, coordinating sales, making personal in-store appearances, and attending annual trade shows in Las Vegas and New York. Jaylen and Nancy, her sisters, were the designers.

One of Marissa's favorite personal appearances was to Goodspell, a high-end specialty clothing and accessory shop in Columbus, Ohio. She was very fond of the owners, Lou and Chris Goodspell, who always treated her well during her trunk show visits. Marissa often asked Andrew to accompany her to Columbus, and the trips doubled as weekend getaways. Ahead of one such trunk show, Andrew agreed to tag along, with one condition: They attend an Ohio State football game. Marissa asked the Goodspells about finding tickets.

The game in question was Ohio State vs. Michigan—one the greatest rivalries in college sports. It was sure to be a true spectacle. The Goodspells managed to secure tickets for Andrew and Marissa, who arrived in Columbus on Thursday night. Though hotel rooms had been difficult to find, they had managed to secure a room at the Scarlet and Gray Inn, a boutique hotel named after the school's colors. On Friday morning, Lou and Chris arrived at 8:30 to drive Marissa to the store, and Andrew drove the rented Camry to the Nationwide Children's Hospital to visit his colleague and friend Gary Pomerantz, the head of pediatric oncology.

It was an enjoyable day for Andrew, and Marissa was a huge success at the store. That night, they shared an excellent dinner at the Capital Steak House with Lou and Chris, and everyone was in a great mood anticipating Saturday's game.

Saturday started early. It was a beautiful, crisp day in late fall, and excitement was in the air. Andrew drove Marissa to the store for an 8 o'clock opening with coffee, scones, and croissants. The store was busy, and practically everyone was dressed in Ohio State's scarlet and gray.

Lou asked Andrew if he would like to do some shopping. "Choose anything in the store—40 percent off!"

Goodspell had a wide selection of fashionable European designer clothing for men. Andrew selected a copper-colored Haupf winter outerwear jacket, a dark blue Armani suit with subtle pinstripes, and a matching Hermès tie. Lou was thrilled. The consummate host, he told Andrew to take another 10 percent off. Before long, it was time to head to the game—the store was empty by noon anyway—and everyone was in excellent spirits. Go Buckeyes, Go!

Fans were everywhere, moving like a single massive, waving organism toward the stadium. Andrew and Marissa drove to the stadium with the Goodspells in their black Range Rover. Lou and Chris were both Ohio State grads and fans, with VIP parking and excellent seats on the 40-yard line, 30 rows up from the field on the Buckeye side behind the scarlet and gray bench. Merely being in the stadium was exhilarating, with more than 101,000 scarlet-and-gray-clad fans chanting, "*Fuck Michigan!*" So much for decorum.

The game itself was a nail-biter. Though she didn't care much for football, even Marissa got into the spirit, clinging to Andrew's arm during moments of tension. After one particularly thrilling touchdown, she jumped up and down and kissed him feverishly. He had never been more in love with her—with anyone really.

The Buckeyes outlasted the Michigan Wolverines, the final score reading 28 to 26. Buckeyes poured onto the field, and pandemonium ensued. With a national championship in sight and a number one ranking conceivable, the fans were rabid. Everyone returned to the store, and Champagne was poured all around. It had been a once-in-a-lifetime experience, truly incredible.

"That's a lovely story," Ginnie said, "but I'm curious why you chose to share it."

"I just wanted to share a story that showed the heart of our relationship," Andrew replied. "For the most part, our time together is truly joyful. We enjoy one another's company and the routine of our daily lives, but we also love to adventure and have fun. Marissa is a wonderful, loving partner. She's caring and calm." He hesitated before adding, "She really puts up with a lot."

Ginnie nodded. "It is clear to me that you have a strong relationship, and that it's one you both value. I believe that uncovering the underlying triggers within your relationship driving you to anger will be immensely helpful in strengthening your marriage in the long term. Were you able to identify anything?"

Ripping off the Band-Aid, Andrew first shared his annoyance with his diet, then his issues with Marissa's lateness.

"It's funny," he said to Ginnie. "I had never really thought about how similar my behavior is to my father's. He used to lose it when my mother was late—and she was late all the time. Just like Marissa."

"That is very interesting," Ginnie agreed, making some notes in her pad. "Tell me more about your father. What was he like? Did he have a temper?"

Andrew explained that his dad's fuse was short, and his actions, at times, were violent. Andrew looked exactly like his father, and his behavior, at least his noxious behavior, mirrored his father's as well. His cousin Beth referred to his father as her "angry Uncle Nate." It did not take much to set him off and send him out of control. Though his father had never raised a hand to anyone in his family, his rages were nevertheless terrifying.

One morning, Nathan lost his temper because Andrew and his sister Maggie were fighting about who would use their shared bathroom first. Nate exploded. He ranted and raved, ultimately punching the wall and breaking his hand. When he returned home that night, he sported a cast from his right forearm to his fingertips.

Ginnie looked contemplative. "And how did your mother react in these instances of your father's rage? Was it similar to how Marissa responds to you?"

Andrew told Dr. Parvich that his mother Ruth had recently passed away at 98. She was a beautiful woman, caring, thoughtful—not perfect, but close to it. She always put the well-being of others, especially her children, before her own. Just as Marissa's maternal instincts were to protect Pia and Serge, Ruth's instincts were to protect Andrew and Maggie. She rarely, if ever, confronted Nate, instead letting him defuse and calm down by himself when he was ready and able to do so. Her approach seemed to work for them.

"And Marissa?"

"Well," Andrew told Ginnie, "Marissa's response to my outbursts are generally quite similar to Ruth's." Marissa did not react, he explained. She withdrew rather than confront him. He could be in the midst of a tantrum and Marissa would turn mute and silently leave the room. Her ability to be noncombative and nonprovocative initially heightened his anger. Eventually though, once Andrew was alone, he would begin to calm down—sit on the wall, eyes closed, deep breaths.

Ginnie suggested to Andrew that he now had another tool—withdrawal. During a triggering incident, she suggested that he remove himself, creating physical distance between himself and the source of his anger.

"Take a step back, close your eyes, and breathe."

Andrew understood, knowing that the real challenge lay in the application of these techniques. If he felt his anger start to build, would he have the wherewithal to remember these new tools? That was the question.

"I've been doing some research, and I'm very curious about the idea of an anger gene," Andrew said.

Ginnie nodded. "I can't say that I know much about that. Of course, it would be difficult to untangle how much something like anger is passed down through patterns of behavior as opposed to a true genetic predisposition, but I agree that it's an interesting concept. Clearly, anger runs in your family, whether genetically or through learned behavior."

"Exactly," Andrew said, excited. "I want to continue researching the idea, also the history of anger and how it has been perceived throughout the growth of civilization. I want to learn as much as possible, in addition to the behavioral modification that we're working on together, so that I can really get a handle on this thing and try to change."

"I think that's a great idea."

"Well, why don't you join me?" Andrew asked.

Ginnie paused. Within the context of the University of New York, it was not uncommon for faculty members to render care to one another while maintaining professional working relationships and even friendships. Frankly, it was one of the advantages of being a healthcare provider at an academic institution, and Andrew counted several of his personal physicians as friends. Still, it was slightly different with therapy, and Ginnie knew that she would have to tread lightly.

"Yes," she agreed. "I would be very interested in assisting in your research, but only if you will agree that it comes second to your treatment and commitment to modifying your behavior. If your research and our dynamic around that research interfere with the urgent work we began in this room, I will have to stop." She spoke firmly, but a hint of excitement was noticeable in her voice.

"Agreed," Andrew said. He was excited. He had always been research focused—he was a doctor, after all—and he liked to understand a subject as completely as possible, particularly if it was a subject that pertained to his personal and professional well-being. He felt that this research would broaden his understanding of anger as a whole and, when paired with the individualized, focused work that he and Ginnie had already begun, he had a real shot at overcoming his own angry tendencies.

Ginnie told Andrew she knew a neurobiologist, Stergios Dimutri, whose research interests encompassed the genetic underpinnings of functional neurotransmitters in the brain. She suggested that she contact Dimutri and solicit his assistance in their quest to understand the rudimentary components of anger.

They shook hands, and Andrew left feeling rather invigorated.

CHAPTER 7

WHO MAKES THE RULES?

Buzzing from his session with Ginnie and the flat white he had picked up on his way out, Andrew decided to give Jeff Flack a call to update him on his progress. Andrew told his boss that he was relieved to be back and thrilled to be seeing patients. Patient care had defined his professional career, and the forced hiatus had been torture, he explained. He also told Jeff that he had seen the ombudsman, Dara Klein, as Dean Smith had suggested. Although he had enjoyed the conversation, she was not part of the reconciliation he needed.

More importantly, he was seeing Ginnie Parvich, a senior member of the Department of Psychiatry in individual behavior modification therapy. He was optimistic that progress would be made, tools learned, and conduct in the face of adversity altered. He asked Flack if, in view of his initiative to seek psychotherapy, the distressed physician course would be necessary.

Flack responded apologetically. "Yes, we've agreed that it is an important part of the process. I think it will be helpful for you, and it will help everyone here to feel better about the situation. The department will reimburse your enrollment, registration, air travel, hotel, and rental car. Just do it."

Andrew felt the familiar pangs of irritation. Why should he have to do the course when he was already working on his own? Shouldn't he know, better than anyone else, what he needed? It didn't even seem like Flack thought it was important, it just seemed like he was checking a box. However, Andrew knew that he was still in a somewhat precarious situation with his employer and arguing would be ill-advised.

He took a deep, steadying breath and replied, "All right, Jeff. I'll let you know when I've made the arrangements."

Shortly after hanging up with Flack, Andrew received an email from Barry Steinglass requesting he make an appointment to meet. He called Steinglass's office, and his assistant said, "He's free now. By chance can you come up?"

"Sure, tell me where you're located. I'll be right there."

Andrew arrived at the 15th floor executive suite offices of the University of New York Hospital building. The entire floor had recently been renovated. There was a central circular lounge that surrounded the elevator bank. Emanating from the core, like spokes in a wheel, were four corridors, three of which contained offices, and the fourth, the executive conference room. The dark wood floor of the central reception area was in stark contrast to the plush, rich blue-gray mohair carpet that covered the corridors.

"You must be Dr. Brown," the receptionist said, smiling. "I'll let Barry know you're here."

A moment later, Barry Steinglass greeted Andrew and shook his hand. "So, how are you doing?"

Brown told Barry that he was well—relieved the ordeal was over. Steinglass apologized for the length of the investigation, reiterating that administration essentially comes to a standstill in August. "I wish that weren't the case, but it's the reality. Everyone's off on vacation."

Steinglass thanked Brown for his patience and apologized again.

He told Andrew that he understood that he had agreed to attend the distressed physician course and had begun to see a behavioral therapist. "Good for you," he said. "You're doing the right thing."

The discussion between Barry and Andrew was collegial. Andrew figured if he were ever going to tell anyone how he felt about the ordeal and the administrative timeout, now was the time. He told Barry it was not the length of time it took to resolve the predicament that troubled him, it was the process itself. He told Barry he felt that the procedure was unfair from its inception. While he appreciated the fact that an employee has the right to levy charges against another and remain anonymous without fear of retribution, it seemed ridiculous for the accused to be left wholly in the dark regarding the offense he or she had ostensibly committed. The University of New York's system acted on the assumption that the accused was guilty, a paradigm contrary to one of the nation's foundational principles. Andrew explained to Steinglass that he felt he had not been afforded his basic rights.

"Tell me, where is the fairness in this process?"

Steinglass had no answer. Still, Andrew was glad to have unburdened himself and to have done so in a more calm and rational manner than he might once have. Perhaps his work with Dr. Parvich was already beginning to have an effect.

CHAPTER 8

ANGER GENE

"There's a question that's been on my mind since last week when we were discussing the potential genetic origins of anger," Andrew began as he took his seat across from Ginnie at their next meeting. "In your opinion, is a tendency toward anger or rage a psychiatric illness?"

Ginnie stood, walked behind her desk, and turned on her computer. She opened the DSM-5, the *Diagnostic and Statistical Manual of Mental Disorders*, a publication of the American Psychiatric Association that served as the Bible for the classification of mental illnesses. She searched the handbook for anger and rage but found nothing specific. There were, however, commonly used associated diagnoses, including oppositional defiant disorder, attention deficit hyperactivity disorder, narcissistic personality disorder, and the one that most closely aligned with anger—impulse control disorder. The latter was characterized by an inability to resist aggressive impulses resulting in assaultive acts and intermittent explosive behavior. Of all the DSM diagnoses, this one came closest to describing Andrew's experience.

Dr. Parvich asked Andrew how he had been since their last session a week ago. "Anything of note? Any inciting incidents, triggers?"

Andrew mentioned that he had spoken with both Jeff Flack and Barry Steinglass. He told her that despite his hesitation, Flack had insisted that he register for one of the distressed physician courses, either in Gainesville at the University of Florida or Nashville at Carter Singer University. He told her he was inclined to go to Tennessee. Neither he nor Marissa had visited Nashville, though they'd heard the city had great restaurants and entertainment. Marissa had agreed to join him in the Music City, but had no interest in Gainesville. Easy, decision made.

"And your meeting with Steinglass?"

"It was all right," Andrew said. "He's a nice enough guy, very apologetic for the delay in reconciliation, but not a rainmaker. He's a company man."

Andrew told Ginnie that when he'd discussed the issue of process and being left in the dark for an entire month regarding the allegations levied, Steinglass had no real response or answer. This continued to trouble Andrew greatly—it seemed unconstitutional, contrary to his inalienable right to be deemed innocent until proven guilty. It would have been different had he not been placed on an administrative hold and been prevented from fulfilling his obligations, particularly to his patients, during the investigative process.

He told Dr. Parvich that he hoped to challenge the University of New York's policy as it existed. He believed he had the reputation and ability to do this—his accomplishments spanned more than 25 years of service, and his good name was known throughout the university. But this would, of course, be in the future. Now was not the time. He would wait and be patient. The window of opportunity would not shut. He believed time to be on his side.

Brown told Ginnie that he had read about the possible hereditary nature of anger. His father's family had a long history of a lack of impulse control. Whether that was genetic, the result of family culture, or some combination of both was unclear, but no one could deny the lineage of rage in the family ancestry.

Scientists who studied the subject reported that one of the strongest inherited genetic traits is temperament, composed of emotionality, activity level, and sociability. Emotionality is defined by how easily someone is provoked or displays anger in upsetting situations. Studies inform that half of our emotionality is inherited. The other half comes from where we live and how we're raised, the influence of environment. Andrew found solace in the belief that anger often runs in families—that he was the product of angry people, that his temper was less a personal failure than a genetic inheritance.

Certainly, he reasoned, genes must be involved in anger, from what makes one mad, to getting mad, to getting over being mad. Anger happens when a stimulus causes chemicals to be released in the brain. The chemicals direct the body to respond physiologically. The reaction begins in the amygdala, the part of the brain responsible for emotions, including anger and fear. The amygdala then sends signals to the hypothalamus, which stimulates the autonomic nervous system consisting of the sympathetic and parasympathetic nervous system. The two function in a complementary, yet contradictory fashion.

The sympathetic system increases the heart rate, blood pressure, and respiratory rate; heightens vision and hearing; and causes the skin to become sweaty and cold. The parasympathetic nervous system is responsible for rest and relaxation, basically undoing the work of sympathetic division. The parasympathetic nervous system decreases respiration, heart rate, and blood pressure. It functions to restore homeostasis and is active when the body is at rest and recuperating.

"So, here we are," Andrew said. "Certainly, there seems to be a genetic predisposition to anger, but environment similarly contributes. Without a doubt, the fact that my father had an explosive temper must be contributing to the inheritance of the anger gene. Frankly," he continued, "I got hit with a double whammy: genes and an ecosystem that normalized anger as part of life."

Ginnie pondered the proposition of an interaction of genetics and environment as etiological predisposing factors of anger and rage. Andrew mentioned that the intersection of family history and lifestyle choices was relevant in the causation of a multitude of diseases and disorders, including heart disease, obesity, and diabetes, to name a few—the list was long. Why not anger? An inherited component and the milieu of our surroundings—home, school, friends, events, and observations—all contribute to behavior, good and bad. Andrew believed that it was fair to conclude that his anger and rage similarly resided at that same intersection.

Ginnie asked if he could recall an incident of anger, an outburst of rage from his childhood. Andrew's eyes widened, his immediate reaction telling Ginnie that he hadn't had to dig deep for an example to share.

Andrew was raised in Merrick, a town on the South Shore of Long Island, he told Ginnie. It was a wonderful place filled with many friends, safety, freedom, and four-season sports at the Smith Street School, located within walking distance of the Brown home. Andrew told Ginnie that when was eight years old, he tried out for the town Little League and was selected for the Yankees, for whom he played second base. During his first year on the team, he did not have a single base hit—25 walks, 3 strikeouts. He smiled thinking about the coarse white wool, pinstriped uniforms. They were so itchy and uncomfortable that his mother Ruth even installed a silk lining in the pants to make them bearable.

As he got older, he became a better baseball player, moved to shortstop, and was a decent hitter—not great, but good enough. When he was 12 years old, he was chosen for the town all-star team. Scheduled games were on Saturday afternoons against teams from Seaford, Rockville Center, and Valley Stream. The winners advanced and the losers went home, a single elimination format. The tournament involved teams from every town, large and small from across the entire country, as well as international teams from Japan and Taiwan. The eight regional winners from New England, mid-Atlantic, South, West, and other regions convened in the annual Little League World Series in Williamsport, Pennsylvania. It was very competitive but still a fun-filled experience.

The Merrick team won their first three games. The fourth, against Hicksville, the Long Island champions from the previous season, was played at the Jones Beach Stadium under the lights. The setting was perfect and the mid-June evening memorable, with a cool breeze permeating the stadium from the nearby ocean. Jones Beach, a New York state park, was a treasure with clean, safe oceanfront beaches, an amusement park, an immense outdoor pool, a nine-hole par-three golf course, a boardwalk, an outdoor summer theater, and two baseball stadiums—one for Little Leaguers and the second a full-size field for games played by high school teams and adult leagues.

The evening of the game was electric. The stadium lights illuminated the field, and the bleachers were filled with parents, brothers, sisters, friends, and onlookers out for an evening stroll on the boardwalk eating hot dogs and ice cream.

At 7 o'clock, the announcer welcomed the fans and Little Leaguers from Merrick and Hicksville. Andrew recalled that his team was arbitrarily chosen as the home team. The players and coaches lined up along the first-base line. Hicksville, the visiting team, took their places on the third-base side of the field. The announcer introduced the starting lineups: "At shortstop for Merrick, Andrew Brown." An American flag was hoisted up the flagpole as "The Star-Spangled Banner" played on the public address system. Cheers erupted from the crowd as the umpire shouted, "Play ball!"

The game was close, dominated by the pitchers. Andrew remembered the Hicksville pitcher was a big, strong, left-handed flamethrower, not to mention the mustache above his upper lip. Twelve years old—really! He threw fastball after fastball, no curves, no changeups, just smoking heat.

Andrew told Parvich that he beat out an infield grounder for a single his first at-bat. When he came to the plate in the fourth inning, Hicksville had a 1-0 lead, but young Andrew dug in—his team desperately needed a hit. Could he deliver and be a hero?

But he struck out on three fastballs. Andrew lost his composure, and rage prevailed. He stomped his feet, threw his bat at the dugout, and shouted, "*Shit!*"

Fortunately, no one was hurt—the dugout fence prevented the bat from striking a teammate. The crowd, however, was shaken and quiet. The cheerful mood had suddenly shifted. The umpire immediately threw Andrew out of the game.

He was humiliated, but there was no place to hide as he sobbed uncontrollably.

"Ginnie, I was only 12 years old. Little did I realize that a pattern of rage and embarrassment, followed by contrition, was to become my future."

Brown recognized the path forward more clearly than ever.

Success would involve overcoming both a hereditary predisposition and learned behaviors cemented from childhood. These components would have to be controlled, though how to separate one from the other would surely pose a challenge. He may have been aware of their unique existences, but how to unravel one from the other in a lifetime of repeated behaviors? That would be difficult.

When considering life expectancy, genetics contribute between 40 and 50 percent. The remainder is dependent on life choices such as smoking, alcohol use, sun exposure, diet, weight control, exercise, and sleep. Tobacco use significantly increases the risk of cancer, heart disease, and stroke. Evidence exists that a single drink or glass of wine may actually be beneficial, while excessive exposure to the sun is not, increasing the risk of skin cancers and melanoma significantly. The Mediterranean diet of fish, beans, vegetables, and fruits is healthy, whereas fatty meat is not. Daily exercise and ample sleep are important as well.

With respect to these factors, Andrew's lifestyle was one to be admired. He abstained from tobacco and alcohol, got regular exercise and plenty of sleep, and routinely used sunscreen. He was diligent—even compulsive—about medical care and generally took his health seriously. While considering his lifestyle choices, it occurred to him that his focus had been largely on cancer prevention. He had not applied the same attention to those factors that might be contributing to his poor emotional health, particularly his tendency toward rage.

Parvich understood that Andrew was a logical thinker, a fixer—a doctor. He needed a concrete plan of action, a lifestyle prescription similar to the one he'd given himself to stay healthy and avoid cancer, but aimed at helping him to avoid anger. Determining the specifics would not be easy, she told Andrew, but if they worked together, the goal was achievable.

She stood, walked to the whiteboard, retrieved a marker, and drew a graph with an X- and Y-axis labeled "time" and "events," respectively. She explained that events represent triggers and responses, and that time referred to how rapidly the anger response escalated. Ginnie told Andrew the first and most important things to recognize were triggers.

"What precipitates your anger?" She told him to focus on the present and future rather than rehash the past. She suggested that he not only contemplate inciting events at home with Marissa, but at work as well. Clearly the repercussions of anger in the office had lasting consequences—understanding those triggers was vital. For each incident, Ginnie wanted him to answer the questions: who?, what?, and where? She told him to recall incidents and imagine his reactions—appropriate or not, civil or not, evoking temper or not. Hard to do, but a must if he hoped to change.

"Andrew, does anything come to mind that we can discuss?"

"To be honest, there is an ongoing and often repeated situation that really pisses me off."

Andrew explained that patients with leukemia needed frequent lumbar punctures to administer intrathecal chemotherapy directly into the cerebrospinal fluid (CSF). The prophylactic spinal taps destroyed existing leukemic blast cells in the CSF and served to prevent their entry into the fluid surrounding the spinal canal and brain, a reservoir site, from the bloodstream. Recognition of leukemic blast cells in the spinal fluid and the need to eradicate them and/or prevent their entry into the central nervous system had proved to be among the most important therapeutic advances responsible for the improved prognosis of children with acute lymphoblastic leukemia.

Years ago, when children needed a lumbar puncture with the instillation of chemotherapy directly into the CSF, a nurse would position the patient on their side, draw their legs to their chest, and hold them down while they writhed in excruciating pain, screaming bloody murder. It was barbaric. Over the last 15 or 20 years, however, it had become common practice to use conscious sedation—intravenous Versed and Demerol—to induce sufficient drowsiness and tranquility to allow the test to be performed quickly and safely with minimal pain to the patient.

The procedure took only five minutes from beginning to end, but during that time the patient required monitoring, suction, potentially oxygen, and a place to recover from the effects of the sedation. The Joint Commission— the hospital accreditation board—mandated more stringent guidelines in the name of patient safety, but the requirements forced the oncology team to perform the procedures in a procedure suite or operating room. The mandated change required the tests be scheduled for a given date and time, since patients could not eat or drink anything up to six hours beforehand and had to be evaluated by Anesthesiology. The ordeal now took 60 or 90 minutes instead of 5 to 10.

In accordance with the requirement that nothing at the University of New York be easy, seamless, or efficient, there was always an issue scheduling cases in the procedure room. Other clinical services similarly needed time: gastroenterology for endoscopy procedures, ENT for eustachian tube placement, rehab medicine for Botox injections needed to correct spasticity, oral surgery for dental extractions. The operating room administration of the Rose Children's Hospital decided the most equitable practice would be to offer each service a block of time. Oncology's assigned allocation was from 12 to 2 p.m.

Brown argued strenuously. His point was that the oncology patients were often infants and small children, and to keep them NPO—no food or water—for six hours, especially when the leukemic kids were on steroids (which enhance appetite) was near criminal. He felt compelled to advocate for the patients and found himself at odds with the charge nurse more often than not. This predicament was a constant irritant.

Andrew told Ginnie he often raised his voice, ranting and raving in view of the public in the clinic workroom. His anger, although altruistic on behalf of his patients, was nevertheless inappropriate, and Andrew knew it. Though his intentions were pure, his approach was flawed, and in retrospect, he always felt terrible. There was no need for him to berate Gail Connors, the charge nurse in the procedure suite—she did not set the policy or make the rules. And ultimately, his temper would negatively impact his patients.

"This is a perfect example of the first step," Parvich said. She told Andrew that his recognition of wrongdoing was important. "When this situation occurs again—and it seems as though it happens frequently—try the following: Stand up, leave the workroom, and do not under any circumstances use the phone. Not a landline and not your mobile. Keep it in your pocket. If need be, ask the nurse practitioners for assistance—no phone calls. Avoidance, avoidance, avoidance.

"In fact, think back to how your mother responded to your father's outbursts, or how Marissa reacts to you—she leaves the room, departs the scene. No confrontation…*avoidance, avoidance, avoidance.*"

Ginnie went to the whiteboard and began to draw. "As a trigger begins to fester, the first reaction is the most important. Try to blunt the trigger immediately by not allowing it to enter your space."

"Okay," Andrew told her. "I'll try."

"Just practice," Ginnie said. "This won't be immediate. For now, I want you to focus on recognizing the trigger and taking that first step of walking away. It may not happen on the first try. You may lose your temper, and that's okay. Don't get discouraged; we're focused on the big picture."

Ginnie told Andrew that she had emailed Dr. Dimutri, the doctor she had mentioned during their last session, regarding their research into the origins of anger, and had asked him to recommend original published articles. She would forward the list to Andrew.

"In the meantime, I've been doing some research of my own," she said.

Ginnie had learned that people who are genetically predisposed toward aggression apparently have increased difficulty controlling their anger secondary to inefficient functioning of the parts of the brain that govern

cognitive-emotional control, and emotional arousal. Aggressiveness and anger seemed to be highly heritable and traceable to abnormalities or dysfunction in the monoamine oxidase-A gene. Located on the short arm of the X, or male, sex chromosome, the monoamine oxidase-A gene has been associated with a variety of other psychiatric disorders and antisocial behavior. It has been demonstrated that a deficiency or absence of the gene results a rare genetic disorder characterized by lower-than-average IQ, problematic impulsive behavior, hypersexuality, violence, sleep disorders, and mood swings.

The MAO-A gene encodes the enzyme monoamine oxidase-A that functions as a pivotal regulator of brain function through its effects on neurotransmitters such as dopamine, norepinephrine, and serotonin. There is an association between low activity of the gene and autism, aggression, panic disorders, bipolar affective disorders, depression, and attention deficit hyperactivity disorders. A connection between decreased gene levels and low dopamine turnover rates when accompanied with high testosterone levels, low socioeconomic standards, and low intelligence predicts violent, aggressive actions and antisocial behavior in men.

The MAO-A gene is also referred to as the "warrior gene." If confronted with social exclusion or ostracism, individuals with the low-activity MAO-A variants showed higher levels of aggression than individuals with the high-activity MAO-A gene. Low MAO-A enzyme activity foretells aggressive male behavior when individuals are provoked. However, without precipitating factors aberrant behavior was less likely to occur.

"There is a difference in MAO-A activity by gender," Ginnie said. "Men who are more prone to commit acts of violence and temper have either a high-functioning or low-functioning version of the gene, whereas women have an intermediate level."

"This is fascinating stuff. I'd like to hear what Dr. Dimutri thinks about it. Think he'd be game for lunch?"

CHAPTER 9

DIMUTRI

Andrew Brown suggested they meet Dr. Dimutri near the main campus of the University of New York, as the choice of restaurants was significantly more varied than the storefront bodegas, diners, pizzerias, and fast-food chains near the medical center. Besides, they all agreed, the quasi-outing to the campus with its students and treeline quad would be a welcome change of scenery.

The university proper, like the medical school to the north, was an eclectic assortment of buildings occupying more than 40 acres of prime West Side real estate. The Baskin Library and domed Little Smith Administration Building were Greek Revival granite architectural masterpieces replete with white columns, located on opposite ends of the quad-anchored college walk. The Chu Engineering Building, Masquard Computer Science Center, and Charles Athletic Complex were modern steel and glass structures. The campus was beautiful, and Andrew welcomed any opportunity to visit.

Andrew made a reservation for three at Local, a favorite eatery that served fresh, organic fare. He and Ginnie took the subway together, having planned their weekly therapy session to follow lunch with Stergios Dimutri. They exited at the University of New York West Side campus and made their way across the street. As they entered the bistro and approached the maître d' station, Ginnie noticed Stergios and waved.

Stergios was a strikingly handsome man. Tall and fit with thick, curly black hair and a tanned Mediterranean complexion that suggested perpetual vacation, he possessed a particularly European confidence. He wore a stylish European suit, a blue shirt, and no tie.

Stergios was born and raised in Larisa, a city of 250,000 about a three-hour drive from Athens. He had a twin sister, Athena, and an older brother, Constantine. Stergios's father Christos and his brother Nikos were both physicians. However, after the death of Christos's father at the hands of the Nazis during World War II, Christos left medicine to run the 300-acre family farm, which sat in the shadows of Mount Olympus. After the war, 22-year-old Christos joined the Greek Army and fought for his country's freedom from the Communists, whose presence and influence were rapidly expanding through Eastern Europe and the Crimean Peninsula. In the 1960s, Christos became mayor of Larisa. He was respected and adored by his friends, neighbors, and countrymen for his fairness and integrity.

As children, the three Dimutri kids worked the farm, growing cotton and corn, raising livestock, milking cows and sheep, and making cheese. His mother Isabella worked at the Larisa University Hospital as a labor and delivery nurse. Stergios and Constantine both studied medicine at the Aristotle University of Thessaloniki. Constantine pursued a career as a general surgeon and remained in Larisa, while Stergios chose a career path as a neurobiologist. He emigrated to the United States and studied at Boston Children's Hospital and Memorial Sloan Kettering in New York City. Though he briefly considered a path in oncology, he became fascinated by neurology when he was introduced to brain connectivity and circuitry in the laboratory of Kenneth Ericson, a Nobel laureate. He decided to devote his efforts to research, and reluctantly relinquished patient care.

After completing his investigative studies in the United States, Stergios returned to Europe to be nearer to his beloved family in Larisa. His siblings tried to convince him to return to Greece, the birthplace of civilization, democracy, and medicine, but instead he accepted a position at the Royal Marsden Hospital in London, founded in 1851 as the first institution in the world dedicated to the study and treatment of cancer—a perfect opportunity.

His time in London proved to be extraordinary. Stergios visited his family frequently, not only in Larisa, but often met Constantine and Athena in Paris or Rome for the weekend. Athena worked in finance and had a position at the Piraeus Bank, a large multinational bank where she served as a consultant to the Greek government during the 2010 financial crisis. Constantine had a similarly respected career and became the chief of the surgery department at the Thessaloniki University Hospital. Stergios merged his knowledge of the brain and the blood-brain barrier to develop a novel delivery system for precision, targeted chemotherapy and immunotherapy agents administered directly into malignant tumors using an infusion pump. Genius, really.

One evening while out to dinner at a pub in Kensington, Stergios met Liani Akhlamathi, an Iranian expatriate whose family had left Iran to avoid persecution from the Muslim fundamentalists who had seized control of the government. Liani, a dental student at Kings College, was smitten with Stergios. They dated, moved in together, and were soon married, deciding not long after to relocate to the United States. Stergios was recruited to the University of New York, where he remained on the faculty for more than 10 years. He was a revered research scientist, a popular mentor and teacher, and a warm, congenial colleague. Liani accepted a position in the university's dental school. The Dimutri family quickly acclimated to New York. Professionally and personally, it worked.

"Greetings, Stergios," Ginnie said. "Let me introduce you to Andrew Brown."

Stergios extended his hand to Andrew, who shook it firmly, saying, "Great to meet you, Stergios. Thank you for agreeing to meet with us. We really appreciate it."

"My pleasure."

The maître d' ushered the trio to a booth along the wall and placed three menus on the table. "Bon appétit."

They ordered drinks—Brown and Parvich decided on Virgin Marys, and Dimutri chose a glass of Sauvignon Blanc from the Napa Valley. Without revealing personal details, Brown gave Stergios a brief overview of how he and Dr. Parvich had come to meet and outlined their mutual goal to learn the origins and evolution of anger and rage as part of the therapeutic stages for behavior modification. He told Stergios that their research had uncovered the existence of an anger gene linked to monoamine oxidase-A and downstream effects on various neurotransmitters.

Their server, clearly an undergrad at the University of New York, returned with their drinks and took their orders.

Stergios told Brown and Parvich that he was familiar with the concept of MAO-A and its potential role in human temperament, particularly in men. He mentioned that brain researchers had recently found that the relationship among genes, anger, and aggression was quite complex. He cited a report that confirmed what Andrew and Ginnie already knew; the MAO-A gene did indeed have a robust association with aggression in humans. The report found that men who display aggressive behavior might have a high- or low-functioning version of this gene, and it reiterated the important impact of serotonin and dopamine as regulators of emotions.

He recalled a study that revealed that people who were genetically predisposed toward aggression appeared to have diminished functioning in the brain regions that help to control emotions. Another investigation suggested men with low MAO-A gene functioning are more prone to aggression when provoked. Other studies had found that men with the low-functioning version of the gene are especially likely to engage in violence and antisocial behavior if they were victims of child abuse or experienced an environment of rage as a child.

The server arrived with their meals, but before they began their repast, Stergios had one last thought.

"Although the current perspective is that genetics can influence one's reaction and quickness for anger arousal, it by no means is the sole factor.

There are many different convoluted and sometimes contradictory forces that determine human behaviors and outcomes. Ginnie, I'm sure you'll agree. So, while we may certainly observe a correlation between genetics and a predisposition to rage, it is impossible to say with any real certainty how much influence genetics have over other factors—upbringing, environment, experiences, and so on."

The three paused, ruminating over this information as they ate their food. The conversation took on a lighter, more personal tone. Andrew asked Stergios about his family and where he lived. He told Andrew and Ginnie that he had two daughters, aged nine and six, and lived in Rye, New York. His wife Liani was an Iranian expat and dentist on faculty with the University of New York, specializing in oral health and care of patients undergoing cancer treatment. They had met in London and immigrated to the United States together. Both were now U.S. citizens.

"What about you?" Dimutri asked Ginnie. "Where do you live?"

"The Upper West Side," she said, but she did not elaborate.

It was a complicated dance she and Andrew were engaging in. Traditionally, he knew therapists and psychiatrists were closed books to their patients, refusing to share personal details in order to avoid boundary crossing or transference. With Andrew, though, the situation was slightly different. They weren't simply doctor and patient, they were also doctor and doctor—colleagues in their quest to better understand the origins of rage. Still, Andrew respected her personal boundaries. He was grateful for her expertise, trust, and companionship and eager to avoid anything that threatened her professional boundaries.

"Marissa and I have an apartment in Dobbs Ferry to be close to the hospital and grandchildren, who live nearby, but really, we consider Rhinebeck home. In fact, we recently made our Hudson Valley address our permanent residence. Have either of you spent much time in the Hudson Valley?"

They said that they hadn't.

"You would love it," he continued. "The spring is especially wonderful, with the trees and flowers in bloom—it's really magnificent. I'd love to have you come spend a day in the country. It's an easy drive, straight up the Taconic Parkway."

The server returned to clear the table. "Dessert or coffee anyone?"

Over cappuccinos, the conversation turned back to Dimutri's research and understanding of the brain and its function. Though it did not specifically involve anger and temperament, he was aware of recent experimental work that implicated competing sections of the brain responsible for

cognitive-emotional control, and another region for emotional arousal. He informed them about a study of healthy college-age men exposed to an anger provoking incident to determine brain reactivity as a function of MAO-A genotype expression as measured by MRI and PET scans.

Male subjects with low gene expression demonstrated increased brain activity after the insult, whereas men with high gene levels did not show enhancement. The investigators concluded that these results suggested that heightened brain activation and their connectivity were neuro-affective mechanisms underlying anger control in participants with the low-functioning levels of the MAO-A gene.

"So, people with the low-functioning variant of the MAO-A gene may be less proficient in controlling anger and aggressive behavior?" Brown asked Dimutri.

Dimutri told Brown he was correct but reiterated his earlier caveat. Though there was an established connection, it was nearly impossible to know how deterministic a genetic predisposition might be when taken in combination with the many other factors that make up a human life and upbringing. Short of running clinical trials from birth, with every factor from home life to relationships controlled, it might never be possible to fully know. What he did know was that it wasn't strong or pervasive enough to be truly determinate. Statistically, he told Brown and Parvich, up to 40 percent of the male population had the low-functioning variant, but clearly only a very tiny fraction of these men will go on to commit serious acts of violence.

Ginnie chimed in that men with the low-functioning variant of the MAO-A gene seemed to have inefficient functioning in the neural circuitry of emotional control. "I wonder if the dysfunction might then predispose people with the low-functioning variant toward aggressive responses to provocation, while people with the high-functioning variant are better able to brush it off."

An interesting thought.

The hour was late, and Stergios told Andrew and Ginnie that he had to get back to his lab.

"We can certainly continue the conversation in the future," he said. "But before I leave, I had one final thought. By identifying genes and brain mechanisms that predispose people to anger and violence, even if the risk is small, scientists may eventually be able to tailor prevention programs to those who need them most."

Dimutri stood and asked Brown if he could pay for his lunch, to which Andrew replied, "Absolutely not. Lunch was my pleasure." Stergios thanked him, and they all shook hands.

As they left the restaurant and crossed the street, Parvich and Brown were silent, processing the conversation they'd had over lunch. They remained silently entrenched in thought during the short subway ride back to the hospital. Back in the psychiatry outpatient building, Andrew did not stop at reception, instead following Ginnie into her office. He took his usual seat, and Ginnie grabbed her notepad.

Ginnie broke the silence, telling Brown that her reading, research, and clinical observation had informed her that, like many aspects of personality, anger consists of a pattern of habits in our thoughts, feelings, and physical sensations. Regardless of whether it is grounded in biology or environment—or a hybrid of both—people develop habits regarding reactions to an inciting trigger. Change requires commitment, patience, and time. She told Andrew she was convinced that individuals with a genetic predisposition toward anger and aggression just have to work harder to overcome their reactivity.

Dr. Parvich confessed that she had not heretofore considered a hereditary component to anger and rage, though she felt it made sense. Regardless of cause, she believed management would be similar. She considered that perhaps the biggest shift would be that if patients with explosive anger see it as a genetic predisposition, they might feel less responsible for their actions. On one hand, this might help to release patients from a cycle of shame and repetition—on the other, they may see it as impossible to overcome.

"I have a question—well, a thought," Andrew interjected. "If MAO-A gene dysfunction is the issue in the low-function population, one might surmise that the level of serotonin—the neurotransmitter needed to stabilize mood and well-being—is similarly low. Why not just replace it to enhance message delivery between nerve cells and prevent violent outbursts and rage? Similar to the way we treat depression, abusive behavior, OCD, PTSD, and other conditions with SSRIs like Prozac, Zoloft, or Paxil in order to increase plasma levels and stabilize mood?" They both sat, considering. "Ginnie, just for the fun of it, Google SSRIs and anger. See if anything comes up."

Ginnie went to the computer and did the search. As expected, several articles appeared touting SSRIs in patients with uncontrolled abusive behavior. She read several case histories aloud, but shook her head as she concluded, "This is not you, Andrew. Your anger, though inappropriate, is still amenable to behavior modification.

"This will be hard—much harder than taking a pill. But I know you're capable of doing the work necessary to change. Anger and rage are existential givens—archetypical human emotions. The issue is not the fact or existence of anger, but how one deals with it, how you reconcile your outbursts. Suppression and repression of anger are counterproductive, fu-

tile, and unhealthy. What is paramount is to accept anger as a natural phe-
nomenon and learn to manage and express it more constructively. In other
words, to modify your behavior.

"The triggers of your outbursts are actually mundane, common matters of
control and frustration," she continued. "They do not seem to be related
to any underlying conditions like depression, alcohol or drug use, or other
psychiatric diagnoses. You don't appear to be overwhelmed by stress, either
at home or work, or by family problems, illness, or financial issues. What
I do recognize in your behavior are characteristics of an intermittent explosive disorder—we commonly refer to it as IED—an entity defined by
repeated episodes of aggressive, impulsive behavior and an overreaction to
a trigger out of proportion to what is realistically warranted. Traditionally,
IED outbreaks last less than 30 minutes and can occur without warning…
Sound familiar?"

Andrew nodded.

"Temper tantrums, fighting, potential for physical violence, throwing
things—these are all common to IED. These episodes are followed by
feelings of intense remorse or embarrassment after the episode has run its
course."

"Wow," Andrew said. "That's—that's exactly it."

Parvich continued. She told Andrew that people with IED tend to present negative, destructive, and dangerous physical side effects alongside the
emotional symptoms. During episodes, adrenaline and cortisol levels increase, elevating blood pressure and heart and respiratory rates and damag-
ing the immune system.

"So it is no exaggeration to say that uncontrolled anger can kill. In the
same way that you monitor your diet and exercise and get regular check-
ups, behavior modification is a necessary step toward ensuring your health
and longevity." She paused for a moment, allowing Andrew to absorb the
information. "Our hour is almost up. I think this has been a very interest-

ing and productive day, and I'm glad to have Dr. Dimutri's perspective as we parse through these complicated ideas.

"Your homework this week is simply to concentrate on avoidance. That means no confrontations—walk away. I suggest that you enlist Marissa's support. Tell her she needs be involved as a watchdog and monitor. Ask her to be on time and to be a partner in your desire to lose weight and diet. But most importantly, should you encounter a spark, douse the fire immediately—walk away, separate."

"I understand," said Brown as he stood to leave. "I agree, our time with Dimutri was invaluable—I'm glad you suggested that we reach out to him. And I hear what you're saying in terms of practical behavior modification—I'm in total agreement—but I can't help but think that I must have inherited the low-functioning variant of the MAO-A gene. I'm not saying there's any need to measure the level or to measure the serotonin in my blood. I do not want to take medication. I trust you and believe that my cure resides in concentrated behavior modification techniques. But given my profession, I can't help but consider the genetics, and to me it does seem clear that in my case, there is a genetic component."

They shook hands, agreeing to continue the conversation the following week. Andrew left the psych building on an emotional high, buzzing with the information he'd gleaned over lunch and during his time with Dr. Parvich. For the first time since his administrative suspension, he felt hopeful.

CHAPTER 10

JUST GO

The week that followed was uneventful, with no upheaval to speak of.

On Sunday evening, Andrew and Marissa prepared a simple dinner of ramen noodles with fennel and bok choy in a lemongrass broth. Andrew set the table for two on the porch of their home in Rhinebeck. The conversation was light and contemplative. Quiet prevailed until Andrew mentioned that Ginnie had recommended Marissa be involved in his recovery. "Honey, please help me. Be my supervisor, my overseer."

Andrew explained that they'd come to the conclusion that an important first step in controlling his anger and temper must be avoidance. "This is important—if you notice that I am about to lose control, we must walk away, separate from each other. You go one way, and I need go another. We take some time alone to defuse and decompress."

Marissa said, "I'll do my best. I promise. But you also have to concentrate on not letting yourself lose control. You're the one in charge of yourself, but I'll help. I'm here for you."

* * *

Rather than his usual stroll from the Powell Building to the Psych Institute the following Wednesday, Andrew navigated the medical school campus with haste. In the waiting room, he remained standing—it was all that he could do to keep from pacing—until Dr. Parvich summoned him to her office. Andrew sat in his usual seat. Ginnie went to the whiteboard and picked up a marker. They had a lot of ground to cover. "By the way, did you have a conversation with your wife? How did it go?"

"Okay, I guess. Marissa understood that I need her participation to overcome my demons, but she told me that the hard work was mine alone. Frankly, she's not wrong."

As he spoke, Ginnie was writing four words on the whiteboard in large, sweeping letters: RELAXTION, DEEP BREATHING, VISUALIZATION.

Capping the green dry-erase marker, Ginnie said, "The first technique in counteracting a stressful situation that could become an inciting incident is to promote relaxation. There are a few comprehensive calming techniques will be of great value."

She suggested that, several times a day, Andrew practice deep abdominal breathing for a full minute. "Pull the air all the way into your belly before pushing it completely out again." She demonstrated and had Andrew practice as well.

"Another tactic is to think of a pleasing, calming scene—a mountain stream, the ocean, playing with your grandchildren. Some people find the repetition of a word or short phrase helpful during deep breathing exercises. Have you ever meditated?"

Many years ago, Andrew had studied Transcendental Meditation (TM), a specific form of silent, mantra meditation popularized by Maharishi Mahesh Yogi in India and advocated in the 1960s by the Beatles. He told Ginnie that he had found TM to be a valuable tool but had not meditated in years.

"That's perfect! Definitely give that a try again. I think you'll find it very calming and helpful in our goal."

Something occurred to Andrew. "Might there be a use for acupuncture?" As part of the oncology program, he had developed an integrative therapies initiative, and acupuncture was an important part of what was offered to patients. Andrew told Ginnie that he found wonderful peace in the pressure released by the needles, and suggested that he would speak to the practitioners and arrange for regular sessions two to three times per week.

"Another important component is regular exercise," Ginnie said. "Physical activity reduces the stress response by decreasing stress hormones like adrenaline and cortisol, increasing endorphins, improving calmness, and promoting restful sleep."

Nodding, Andrew said, "Exercise—not a problem."

Andrew told Ginnie that exercise was already a part of his daily routine. He ran regularly in Central Park when he and Marissa lived in Manhattan and continued the routine until the aching in his back and knees became too great. Presently, he used a Peloton bike four to five times per week.

"Perfect!" Ginnie said. "Continue your routine and consider increasing aerobic training to improve your cardiorespiratory function."

"Lastly," she continued, "Maintain your social relationships. Social support can minimize your psychological and physiological reactions to perceived threats. It provides a sense of safety and protection, which makes you feel less fearful and angry. Clearly, your most important friendship is Marissa, but friends and work colleagues are also important."

She returned to the whiteboard and wrote: EXERCISE, SLEEP, SOCIALIZATION.

Andrew felt at ease socially. He made friends easily and enjoyed being with others. "Marissa and I have an active social life—sometimes too active, frankly—but the absolute most important relationships in my life are with Clara and Wes. I know that I'm a significantly better grandparent than I was a parent. No do-overs, but I'm determined not to repeat my old mistakes."

"Understood," Ginnie said. "And I trust that with time and effort, you won't." She paused. "When we first met, I asked how you decompress after an outburst of explosive rage. Do you recall what you told me?"

Andrew nodded. "I sat on the wall, closed my eyes, and took deep breaths."

"Andrew, your challenge is to put this all together. You know what to do—in a way, you've always known. But now you have to apply it. Practice, practice, practice. Your primary goal is to always, if possible, avoid confrontation. However, if a situation triggers rage, sit on the wall—so to speak—close your eyes, and take deep breaths."

"Got it. Easier said than done, but I will do my best."

"Good. Now, there's no guarantee you'll encounter an inciting incident in the next week or even the next two weeks. I think it makes sense to hold off and schedule our next session a month out—that should allow you time to use the new skills you've acquired."

Andrew agreed.

* * *

On his walk back to his office, he called and updated Jeff Flack, saying that he was making great progress and that much to his surprise he was actually enjoying his time with Dr. Parvich.

"I'm in my best element in those sessions," he told his chairman. "I get to become a student. Between sessions, I've been reading about the very nature of anger, its etiology, and its role in genetics and evolution. And most importantly, we've been discussing practical mechanistic techniques to help me prevent any future inappropriateness." He continued, mentioning that he had met Stergios Dimutri, an incredibly knowledgeable scientist who promised to be a future resource.

"I think you'll agree, I've been quite proactive in addressing this situation," Andrew said, hoping his tone sounded more casual than he felt. "Any chance you could give me a pass on the 'distressed physician' course? I really feel that individual therapy—one on one—will be significantly more helpful to me."

Flack sighed. "Listen, Andrew, you know as well as anyone the bureaucracy involved with this place. This isn't just about me," he paused. "Do me a favor, Andrew. Just go."

CHAPTER 11

WELCOME TO NASHVILLE

The decision had been made. Brown had no choice but to start preparing for his unwanted visit to Nashville and the course for distressed physicians at Carter Singer University. Perhaps it was the name of the course that made him so uneasy. He did not think of himself as a distressed or troubled physician, and never had.

On the contrary, he felt better than he had in years. His sessions with Dr. Parvich were going well, and he was confident in the progress they were making. What's more, he could see the ripple effects both at work and in his relationship with Marissa. His health was excellent, his marriage was strong, the children and grandchildren were thriving, work was as successful as ever.

It frustrated him that, even with all the progress he'd made, he was being pushed into this course—it felt like backtracking. But he had no choice—he would simply have to get it over with.

The course's website, a boilerplate of psycho-emotional speak and buzzwords, stated that the course was developed to assist physicians with a history of disruptive behavior directed at colleagues and patients. The prospectus indicated that participants would obtain skills to recognize unprofessional behavior and learn strategies to mitigate harmful behavior in the workplace.

Wasn't that precisely what he was doing with Dr. Parvich?

He scrolled through the site, his irritation spiking when he reached the cost of enrollment—$10,000. Add airfare, hotel, meals, and ground transportation—all said and done, the cost would be $15,000.

Armed with this information, he called Rich Wilson, the department's chief financial officer, to inform him, hoping he'd pull the plug when he learned the full damage. Wilson told him that he would confirm with Jeff Flack and get back to him.

Less than an hour later, an email appeared in Andrew's inbox: *Dr. Flack agreed. The department will pay 100 percent of the cost.*

Wilson said that he would pay the enrollment fee directly and reminded Andrew to retain all his receipts for reimbursement.

Andrew could sense the all-too-familiar feelings of rage beginning to bubble up inside him. He thought of the many children in need of treatment whose parents could hardly afford the ambulance ride to the hospital, let alone treatment and accommodations. To simply throw away $15,000 on a redundant, unnecessary, punitive, and frankly humiliating trip made his blood boil.

He closed his eyes and took a few deep breaths. He sat on his wall. Andrew knew that he needed to relax. The decision was beyond his control.

He texted Ginnie and asked if she could please call his cell. He needed her advice.

"Andrew, its Ginnie, what's going on?"

"I spoke with Flack, and I have no choice here—I have to take the course," he said, struggling to keep his voice under control. "It's a massive waste of time, not to mention money—I mean, fifteen thousand bucks down the drain just so I can do some role playing to make HR feel better."

Ginnie told him to relax. "Slow down. Be calm," she said. "Sit on the wall, close your eyes, and take deep breaths. There's nothing for you to do here.

You love your job, you want to keep it. This is what you need to do to make that happen. Treat this as an opportunity to practice everything we've been working on."

The next morning, as instructed, Brown called the designated phone number at Carter Singer University. He introduced himself to Bill Sugarland, his contact, and inquired about the course that would commence in January. He told the course director that the University of New York would be paying the tuition and provided Rich Wilson's contact information and email address.

A few weeks later, Andrew and Marissa boarded their direct United Airlines flight from Newark to Nashville. At the Nashville International Airport, they rented a Camry and entered the address of their hotel into the navigation system. The hotel was situated on the campus of Carter Singer University, about 45 minutes from the airport.

The 19th-century industrialist Carter Singer had founded the university in Nashville, and its name honored his life and legacy. Originally run by the Methodist Episcopal Church, Carter Singer severed its ties in 1920, expanded its educational offerings to include graduate schools of business, law, and medicine, and became one of the leading private universities in the country.

Night had fallen, and it was dark when they arrived. What they could see of the sprawling campus was beautiful—exceptional for a school in the city. The medical school buildings, the university hospital, and the children's hospital sat adjacent to the main campus, all of which were separated from downtown Nashville by the Cumberland River.

Their 10th-floor room at the University Marriott was sparsely furnished with a king-sized bed and nightstands from IKEA and a Samsung TV atop a double dresser. The large window had a direct view into the university's football stadium, empty in January, but nonetheless exhilarating. Carter Singer was a member of the Southeastern Conference, a powerhouse division that included Georgia, Alabama, and Louisiana State, whose football teams always ranked among the top in the country. One could imagine what it was like on fall days with the stadium packed with fans, students, and marching bands, a spectacle to behold. Ideologically, Carter Singer was more closely aligned academically and athletically to the Ivy League, but the money it generated as a member of the SEC was considerable, and surely influenced its decision to remain a member of the southern alliance.

Brown awoke early the following morning, showered, and dressed without disturbing Marissa, who was still asleep. He drove to the Clarke Office Building on the medical school campus adjacent to the University Hospital and took the elevator to the 12th floor. Marissa would take a car service downtown and spend the day sightseeing and shopping. She had accompanied Andrew as a tourist and looked forward to taking in the restaurants and music venues and visiting new shops and stores.

Andrew was the first to arrive. The conference room was mostly empty, with a large square table and chairs in the center of the room and a whiteboard mounted on the windowless wall. In front of each of the five chairs was a name placard, looseleaf binder, and a softcover volume entitled *The Anger Control Workbook*. Andrew tried not to groan audibly as he placed his belongings and folder at his designated seat.

Breakfast was available on a sideboard, and he helped himself to a yogurt parfait with berries and coffee. Internally, he was steaming. He flat-out did not want to be in Nashville, did not want to be at Carter Singer University Hospital, did not want to be at a course for distressed physicians. He was embarrassed, his stomach was in knots, and his head ached. He contemplated leaving. He could simply walk out. No one would be the wiser.

But just then a voice from the doorway said, "Dr. Brown, I'm Bill Sugarland. Welcome to Carter Singer."

Sugarland was an older man of average height, likely in his late 60s, with white hair and mustache. He was adorned in turquoise jewelry, including a bracelet, ring, belt buckle, and bolo tie. It was certainly…a look. Raised in Oklahoma on a reservation, he was part Cherokee on his father's side.

He had attended Oklahoma State University on a federal scholarship and graduated with a degree in social work. After more than a decade working to provide much-needed social services on the reservation, he had received a master's degree in psychiatric social work from Carter Singer University and was instrumental in developing the distressed physicians course at the request of the chairs of the departments of medicine and psychiatry.

Initially, the program provided service only to Carter Singer faculty, but the enterprise was so successful that Sugarland sought permission to extend the course to troubled professionals from other medical schools. It was well attended and highly regarded, soon becoming an important revenue stream for the university.

Despite his obvious angst, Brown stood out of politeness to shake hands. Sugarland asked if he could call him Andrew, indicating a less formal feel to the space.

"Of course."

Other people—"distressed physicians," Andrew sneered to himself—began to arrive, placing their folders on the table in front of their name placards and serving themselves breakfast. No one spoke a word. Including Brown, there were five participants, all of whom were men—it was very rare for female physicians to enter the course.

"Gentlemen, good morning. I'm Bill Sugarland, your course director. As you're having breakfast, I want to introduce Mike Lawrence, a psychologist here at Carter Singer. He'll be one of the course instructors. Guy Worley from psychiatry, and Beth White, an internist and associate dean for faculty affairs, are joining as well."

Sugarland told them that their binders contained the course syllabus, schedule, and a list of all the lectures. "We will use *The Anger Control Workbook* as supplemental material. It contains homework assignments to be completed each night in preparation for the following day."

Sugarland indicated that he had previously spoken with each registrant and that some were attending voluntarily, while others were here because their institution demanded their participation.

He told the group to look on the bright side for a moment. "Your hospital was willing to pay your hefty tuition. If they had no interest in your future, would they have done so? Probably not. Now, before we begin, please introduce yourselves. Tell us your name, what you do, and where you're from. There will be ample opportunity to learn about the specifics of why you're in the program. Let's start with you."

"Bruce Tyler. I'm a heart surgeon from Pittsburgh."

"Brian Hamilton, Birmingham, Alabama, urology."

"Andrew Brown, pediatric oncologist from the University of New York."

"Alan Chisholm, psychiatrist from Columbus, Ohio."

"Michael Smith, Ann Arbor, cardiologist."

"Gentlemen, before this week is up, you will become a band of brothers. Together we will peel the onion, uncover hidden thoughts, actions, and bad behavior, and learn mitigation strategies. We have a guiding principle: privacy and confidentiality. And we expect each of you to adhere to this standard of silence. Any questions?"

By this time, Andrew, unable to relax, had a countenance of obvious annoyance. He was angry, and it was apparent to the others.

"Dr. Brown, Andrew, do you want to share something with the group?"

"Look, I am really upset." Brown struggled to keep his voice calm. "I don't want to be here. I'm attending under duress. I am not a distressed physician. I said 'fuck,' and someone got offended. And now I'm here. For what?"

"You have two options, Dr. Brown. Cool it or leave. Up to you. I urge you to stay. I'm convinced you'll derive some benefit from being here, but it's your choice. I appreciate how you feel. Honestly, I do. In fact, your position is not unique. We've been doing this course for 20 years. Do you really think no one in all that time has not felt exactly as you do? But you're going to have to calm down."

Brown told the group he felt stigmatized and labeled, saying there was no reason for him to be there.

Beth White, a tall, thin woman of color from Brooklyn who was seated to Andrew's right, added that his situation was quite common. "Give the course a chance," she urged him. "I think you'll find that you benefit from the experience."

Andrew was pissed, but knowing that he had no choice, he relented. "All right…I'll stay."

"Don't do us any favors," Sugarland said firmly. "If you stay, you must be a willing participant. Don't ruin this for the others."

Brown stood, went to the sidebar, poured another cup of coffee, took a sip, and sat back down in his designated chair. He took a deep breath, beginning to relax. "Sorry, guys."

Sugarland opened his laptop and projected a PowerPoint presentation onto the whiteboard. The first slide read: "Course Goals: Accountability, Identify Risk, Skills, Effective Leadership."

Andrew reflected on his sessions with Ginnie Parvich. Nothing new here. Still, he had made a commitment not to ruin this for the others. He would do his best to remain silent and attentive.

One of the slides was "The Serenity Prayer" credited to Reinhold Niebuhr, an American theologian and ethicist. It resonated with Andrew.

Niebuhr wrote about being calm, living and enjoying each day to its fullest, and accepting adversity as a pathway to peace and fulfillment in this life and in the next.

The prayer provided a moment of solace and personal reflection for everyone in the room, the band of brothers and staff alike.

The group then discussed the qualities of a leader and the merits of intelligence quotient (IQ) and technical skills versus emotional intelligence (EQ). Mike Lawrence referred to an article by Daniel Coleman that appeared in the Harvard Business Review in 1998 that concluded the *sine qua non* of leadership is EQ. The corporate world was replete with examples of highly intelligent, skilled executives who, when promoted to positions of leadership, failed miserably due to lacking adequate EQ.

Andrew believed he was the paradigm of a leader with an adequate IQ but an extremely high EQ. He succeeded not because he was smarter than his colleagues but because of his skills with people. He put patients and coworkers first, and never asked anyone to do something he would not do himself. He attributed his ability to recruit and retain talent, mentor his subordinates, and raise philanthropic dollars to his empathy and connection with people.

On the flip side, however, he had an explosive temper and was prone to rage—behavior that had nearly derailed all that he had accomplished. This duality was surely interrelated. Perhaps it was his ability to empathize with and feel the distress of others that caused his anger to spiral out of control. He wondered whether one could exist without the other. Of course, that was what he was here to find out.

"Throughout the day, you'll each have an opportunity to share a little more about yourselves with the group. Let us know what brought you to the course and what you're hoping to get out of your experience here. Bruce, would you like to begin?"

Bruce Tyler was an affable guy. Dressed comfortably in jeans and a black sports coat, he seemed comfortable and at ease in his own skin.

"Well," he began. "I've spent my whole life in Pittsburgh. I grew up in Shadyside, went to undergrad at Carnegie Mellon, and trained as a thoracic surgeon at Pitt Medical School, where I'm still on faculty." He paused, a momentary break in his placid countenance. "I'm also an alcoholic. I got arrested twice for drunk driving and had my privileges suspended after I entered the operating room drunk. I put the lives of my patients at risk and nearly destroyed my family. My wife walked out, threatened divorce, and my two daughters—they're grown up, out of the house—they won't speak to me." He sighed.

"My choice was to make a change or lose everything I've worked for my entire life. I didn't want to admit it, but the truth was I had a problem—*have* a problem. So, I joined AA and started counseling. Each day is another step on the road to recovery. Thank God, there seems to be some hope for redemption. I haven't lost my job, and my wife hasn't filed for divorce. But my department chair insisted that I attend this course before my privileges are reinstated. So here I am."

Bruce looked around the room, making eye contact with the other doctors, who nodded in solidarity. Andrew was impressed. Here was a man who had nearly lost everything: his family, his career, his reputation. Andrew didn't know the circumstances of his alcoholism, how it had begun, or whether it ran in the family, but what he did know was that Bruce was taking responsibility for his actions. He had made the decision to take charge of his life and break a pattern of poor behavior, and he was doing so with honesty and integrity. The group acknowledged Bruce, thanked him for sharing his story, and genuinely wished him success.

"Bruce, thank you for being the first to share your story and for sharing so openly," said Sugarland. "Let's all take a 10-minute break and then we'll reconvene."

As the men stood up to stretch, grab water, and check their cell phones, each individually made their way over to Bruce Tyler. They murmured their support, patting him on the back. There were a few genuine utterances of "Good luck, man," and "I've been there." Perhaps Sugarland was right—they were already beginning to feel like a band of brothers.

When the group reconvened for its next session, the discussion was led by Guy Worley from psychiatry. He told the group that he would be speaking about self-awareness, self-control, empathy, the art of listening, the art of resolving conflict, and the art of cooperation. But first, he paraphrased Aristotle's Challenge about anger.

> *"Anyone can become angry, That is easy…but to be angry, with the right person, to the right degree, at the right time, for the right purpose, and in the right way…That is not easy!"*

Worley's overarching message was to slow down and be CALM: Control, Assess, Lead, Manage. Andrew chuckled to himself—this group sure liked its acronyms.

After Worley's session, it was time to break for lunch. Andrew checked his phone and saw a message from Marissa. With everything going on in the group, he hadn't had a chance to check in with her. Before listening to the message, he called her back.

"Hi, honey. I saw that you called. What's up? Are you all right?"

"Everything's fine," Marissa said, her tone casual but efficient. "I just wanted to let you know that I moved hotels. While I was exploring downtown, I found a beautiful old hotel, the Hermitage, that's walking distance to shopping and restaurants. It's much more charming than the Marriott, and I think it will be a much nicer place to come back to after a long day with the group." She paused, trying to gauge Andrew's mood. For the days leading up to the trip and during their plane ride and journey to the hotel, Andrew had felt like a ticking time bomb, his rage palpable.

"So…how is it, anyway?" She asked, her tone artificially light.

"Not as bad as I thought it would be," Andrew said genuinely. He was distracted, still thinking about Bruce Tyler. "I'm going to give it a chance, at least—I suppose I have to."

"That's great, honey. I'm so happy to hear that!" Marissa's words rushed out of her mouth in a stream of relief that made Andrew feel guilty. He'd been so consumed with his anger, frustration, and humiliation about coming down that he hadn't fully considered how his moods were impacting his wife.

"I've got to get back," he said. "I'll see you about 5:30. Did you make a reservation for dinner?"

"Yep, we're all set. Good luck this afternoon. I'll see you soon. I love you."

Back around the table, Sugarland addressed Dr. Chisholm. "Alan, would you mind taking the next turn and telling us about yourself?"

Chisholm, in his mid-40s, was the youngest member of the group. He appeared to be a stereotypical Midwesterner in polyester and plaid—certainly not a sophisticated look. His long, disheveled brown hair and unshaven jaw completed the look of someone who did not necessarily care about his appearance.

Alan Chisholm practiced psychiatry in Dublin, Ohio, a suburb of Columbus. He had grown up in Kentucky, attended Loyola of Chicago and Creighton University School of Medicine, and had been in Ohio ever since. Chisholm said he had been sued for malpractice by the family of a patient under his care. The patient, a 22-year-old male, was a severely depressed cocaine addict. He had failed to keep appointments, refused to take antidepressants, and had called Alan's answering service incessantly at all hours of the day and night.

"Somehow, he found my mobile phone number and began to call and text me relentlessly," Alan said. "I told him that he had to stop harassing me or I would have no choice but to call the police. It was clear that I couldn't continue treating him. No progress could be made under the circumstances and given the deterioration of our dynamic. When I suggested several other therapists in Dublin or at Ohio State, he told me to go fuck myself."

Two days later the patient's father called Alan to tell him that his son had committed suicide. He held Chisholm responsible for his death and intended to sue. The case was settled, but the state of Ohio temporarily suspended Chisholm's medical license. Part of the conditions for reinstatement dictated that he attend the distressed physicians course. "So, here I am," Alan said, echoing Bruce.

Andrew was in utter disbelief. He closed his eyes, took a deep breath, and thought to himself, *What am I doing here? These guys are in serious trouble.* Bruce had come into the operating room drunk. Alan had gotten embroiled in a legal battle that could have cost him his license, or worse. Andrew felt for the men and wished them the best, but he didn't feel that his own experience was even remotely comparable. How did saying the word "fuck" put him on the same level as someone who'd gotten arrested twice for drunk driving?

Sugarland was speaking again. He told the group that the next session was about understanding family and genealogy, reminding everyone about their commitment to privacy and strict confidentiality regarding this sensitive topic.

"Family patterns have influence and predictive value upon all of our actions and reactions," he said. "The recognition of familial norms is a potent mitigation strategy. The past and present interact."

Brown was paying attention. The conversation echoed the one he'd had with Dr. Parvich. Sugarland continued, discussing the role of nature versus experience. He offered no new information, and Andrew felt his interest wane as his annoyance mounted. This was time that he could have spent with Dr. Parvich doing meaningful work. Instead, he was stuck here with a bunch of guys in serious trouble—guys he couldn't relate to—receiving redundant information. All for the price tag of $15,000. He checked his watch with dismay.

Next, Sugarland explained how to construct a genogram. He demonstrated the use of symbols and connectivity through the generations of a family tree, and posed questions for the group to answer to trace the origins of behavior. He asked each member of the group to think about conflict resolution and describe addiction and serious illness in family members, contemplate values and traditions of importance, the role of religion, and evidence of trauma, be it sexual, physical, or emotional.

The genogram would be easy for Andrew, as he had a small family: one sister, three aunts, one uncle, and six cousins. Anger was prevalent in his father's family, and he knew little about his mother's kinfolk. Long life and health were predominant. Religion was a non-event, and there was little to no history of trauma. Just explosive tempers and rage.

As the lecture concluded, Sugarland said, "An important strategy is to avoid conflict, recognize boundaries, and withdraw rather than be confrontational."

This resonated with Andrew, as it mirrored the mitigation techniques he had practiced with Dr. Parvich—the proverbial wall. Again, he found himself irritated by the redundancy. The whole exercise was useless, a waste of time.

"Gentlemen, before we conclude for the day, let's hear background from one more doctor. Dr. Hamilton, would you mind sharing your story?"

Hamilton stood and walked into the small kitchen adjacent to the conference room. For a moment, Andrew wondered whether he was planning to leave or maybe open the window and jump rather than share his story. But instead, he opened the refrigerator, grabbed a bottle of water, returned to his seat, and cleared his throat. He began by telling the group that he was a Southern boy. Raised in Atlanta, Georgia, he had attended Auburn University in Alabama as an undergrad, where he had played shortstop on the baseball team that went to the NCAA finals and lost to the University of Southern California. He was drafted by the Cleveland Indians, but instead decided to go to medical school at Emory University in Atlanta.

He had completed his residency at the University of Alabama in Birmingham and had been on the faculty more than 25 years. His area of expertise was prostate surgery, especially robotic and minimally invasive surgery for cancer. Hamilton said that he loved operating. If possible, he would be in surgery five days a week, all day. He was considered the top prostate surgeon in the state of Alabama.

Hamilton was the antithesis of Alan Chisholm. Over 6 feet tall with a strong, athletic build, he was well-groomed and well-dressed in an expensive herringbone tweed sports coat and matching dark gray slacks. He had an air of confidence that matched his station and reputation.

Though he loved surgery, other necessities of the job were less compelling to him. He despised administrative duties and tolerated office hours, but he had little tolerance for urology residents who did not share his zeal and work ethic in the operating room.

"When I began my career in urology, it was a male-dominated specialty," he said. "Over the last decade, that's changed. There's an increasing number of women entering urology, and they seem to universally reject diseases and surgery of the prostate in favor of female genitourinary issues and pediatric urology." His tone did not mask his obvious disgust. "They go through the motions," he spat. "No interest, no skills…a lot of bitching and moaning." He paused. "It's clear the female residents dislike being with me as much as I dislike having to be in the OR with them."

Several female colleagues had complained to the chair of his department, saying that he had harassed and spoken to them inappropriately. He had been overly harsh and angry, belittling them publicly and treating them as inferior to male residents. Pending an investigation, the residency program was placed on probation. The senior administration of the hospital, the dean of the medical school, and his chairman had restricted Hamilton's privileges, disallowed any contact with residents and medical students, and demanded he enter counseling and attend the distressed physicians course. "So, I guess I have no choice."

Sugarland thanked Hamilton.

"There is a powerful and important message here regarding what exactly constitutes sexual harassment in the workplace," he told the group. "Most believe that it connotes a solicitation of sex in exchange for favors, advancement, position, et cetera. However, the request for sexual favors is only the tip of the iceberg. Harassment includes exclusion, obscene gestures, hostility, vulgar language, relentless pressure, name-calling, and not giving proper credit for work. Women not being compensated equitably for comparable work to their male colleagues is also a form of harassment."

Hamilton shook his head while the rest of the group looked down at their binders, unsure of how to respond. Andrew felt irritated. The broad strokes of "harassment" were what had gotten him into this mess. Since when had everyone gotten so sensitive? Sure, it sounded like Hamilton was a jerk to work with, but wasn't that part of the job? Now, here he was, $15,000 later…

Andrew recalled his tenure as the director of pediatric oncology and his relationship with the women he hired and mentored. Pediatrics in general, and pediatric oncology specifically, was a popular subspecialty and career choice for female doctors, and 7 of the 11 full-time faculty members were women. Brown recognized that it was important to facilitate a work environment that would allow his colleagues to be successful physician scientists and also to be content and fulfilled at home. His opinion was informed by Marissa, who ran a fashion jewelry company and raised a family. It was difficult but doable under the right circumstances, and he was determined to provide support.

Several of the women asked to work four-day weeks instead of the traditional five, which he had allowed. Routinely, exceptions were made to accommodate busy schedules, but most importantly he nurtured each of his younger colleagues to find a professional niche, something they could own—be an expert, a career-builder.

"This has been a good first day." Sugarland was wrapping things up. "We're peeling that onion. Your homework assignment is in *The Anger Control*

Workbook. And don't forget the genogram. See you in the morning. We'll have breakfast available again."

Andrew bade goodbye to the others and took the elevator to the basement, where the door opened into the garage. He drove his rental car the short drive to the Hermitage Hotel. Marissa was right: The hotel was much better situated, in an elegant old building with a stately lobby and parlor. The hotel had been commissioned by affluent residents of Nashville in 1908 and shared its name with Andrew Jackson's estate. It was built in the Beaux-Arts style and was the only remaining example of this style of architecture in a commercial building in the entire state of Tennessee.

Their room was beautiful and well-appointed, with a plush king-size bed. And their view was of the state capitol building and park. Beyond these comforts, getting off campus provided Andrew with the mental space he needed to process the day's events and hopefully shed some of his frustrations. Here, he could almost imagine that he and Marissa had taken a vacation and were exploring Nashville of their own accord.

Marissa told him that their dinner reservation was at Husk, an award-winning restaurant known for its distinctly Southern cuisine and located in an old mansion in Nashville's historic district.

The food was delicious: hush puppies, catfish, sweet potatoes, and a succulent chocolate cream pie for dessert. Over dinner, Andrew recounted the events of the day, sharing the others' backgrounds, excluding details and names. He gave away just enough information so that he could properly convey how badly he was being treated by Flack and the administration of the University of New York. Again, he repeated that he did not want to be in Nashville, at Carter Singer, at the course for distressed physicians.

Marissa told him to stop complaining and give it a rest. Make the best of the situation.

"You're here. What do you want to do, leave now? Enough."

CHAPTER 12

BAND OF BROTHERS

Andrew and Marissa woke early, dressed, and enjoyed the complimentary breakfast buffet in the parlor at the Hermitage. Andrew had pancakes and bacon, a splurge for certain but infinitely better than the cold, faux Egg McMuffin prepared by the hospital food service. Marissa had an egg white and mushroom omelet, a ginger scone, and coffee. They each took a section of *The Tennessean*, the right-leaning Nashville daily newspaper. It was depressing for New Yorkers to read but provided a window into the minds of some types of Southerners.

Marissa did not have definite plans for the day. She asked the concierge for recommendations for sights to see, a place for a typical Nashville lunch, and shops to browse.

Holding a map and a list of things to do and see, Marissa, wearing comfortable shoes and carrying an umbrella in case of rain, left the hotel with a determined pep to her step. The Country Music Hall of Fame and Museum was at the top of her list of sights. It was a long walk but certainly doable, and besides, the walk would allow her time to take in the color and flavor of the city. Neither Marissa nor Andrew were country music fans, but when in Rome…

Andrew was calm, resigned to be more accepting. He promised his wife that he would be attentive, participatory, and receptive. The short 15-minute drive to Carter Singer was uneventful, with no rush hour traffic to contend and, with only country or Christian music on the radio, silence was preferred. Andrew was the last of the group members to arrive, he took his place at the conference table while the others were enjoying breakfast, immersed in small talk.

Bill Sugarland entered the conference room. "Good morning, everyone. Did y'all enjoy Nashville last night?"

He told the group the schedule for the day would be a review of the genogram project and a discussion about flooding, how to recognize it, and how to stop it in its tracks. Andrew and Michael Smith were on deck to share their stories. After lunch, Sugarland said he wanted to spend some time discussing harassment and hear the group's perspectives and thoughts on the subject. He asked if anyone had any questions before beginning.

Guy Worley began the discussion about family histories, and the band of brothers, thankfully, were not into it. No one had any revealing information to offer, and the conversation fell short. Sugarland recognized the lack of interest and suggested the next topic, flooding. "Mike, take us out."

Mike Lawrence adjusted his laptop and loaded the next lecture. He told the group that flooding was very primitive physiological response to a perceived threat. If one was confronted with danger or an inciting trigger, the first response to stress was to react quickly in self-defense, with the release of the hormones adrenaline and cortisol to the nervous system, generating the "fight or flight" response. The result was to feel emotionally overwhelmed and incapable of processing information. Symptoms included an inability to think, hear, or communicate clearly, and the physiological response of a pounding heart, shallow breathing, and sweaty hands. Flooding often caused a situation to escalate quickly out of control.

Mike indicated that the intensity of the feelings of anger mattered little. Shame and hurt would almost always manifest in a noxious response toward the perceived enemy. He told the group that flooding was different for men and women—the former flood more quickly, and are more easily overwhelmed, staying flooded longer than their female counterparts, who are able to soothe and calm themselves. Once flooded, the affected individual has two options, neither positive nor productive: Fight and become defensive, or flight without resolution.

Mike Lawrence turned to Andrew. "How would you go about handling flooding?"

Andrew recalled the responsive reactions he had discussed with Ginnie. Sit on the wall, close your eyes, and take deep breaths. He answered, "Avoidance and calm."

Bruce Tyler believed the first thing to do was to recognize a trigger. That would hopefully help the afflicted person to take a step back and recognize the reality of the situation.

Mike nodded, adding, "Take time out. Learn the physiological signs of flooding, and stop, take deep breaths. Disengage from unhelpful thoughts while self-soothing. Exercise, listen to music, subtract 7s from a hundred, meditate—whatever works. Take slow, deep breaths, in and out, watching your abdomen rise and fall."

Sugarland intervened and told them that flooding frequently occurs in situations between two people—husband and wife, business partners, parent and child. He mentioned that, following the initial insult or trigger of bad behavior and the cooling-off period, it was necessary to reestablish dialogue and communication. He mentioned that powerful phrases exist to deescalate conflict, the most important, without question, being, "I'm sorry."

One must be able to view the issue from the other's perspective, weigh the pros and cons, and move forward. Mike Lawrence asserted that good communication was the prescription for success, respect, trust, and efficiency.

"But as calm prevails, the conversation should be continued and resolved. If not readdressed, issues fester and flooding may ensue again. Any questions, comments?"

The group offered no reaction.

"Michael, Andrew, who would like the stage to tell their story?"

Michael Smith looked at Andrew. "I'll go."

Michael told his compatriots that he was from Michigan and had been raised in Bloomfield Hills, a suburb of Detroit. His father was a doctor, an internist, and his mother was a pediatrician. He attended the University of Chicago as an undergraduate and attended the University of Michigan for medical school. He stayed on to complete his residency and cardiology fellowship and remained on the faculty full-time. He and his wife, Barbara, and three teenage children, two boys and a girl, lived in Ann Arbor, an idyllic place to raise a family. He was Michigan maize and blue through and through.

Dr. Smith said he limited his practice to interventional cardiology, cardiac catheterizations, stent placement, clot retrieval, and recently, transcatheter aortic valve replacement (TAVR), a minimally invasive procedure to re-place a narrowed aortic valve that failed to open properly.

Smith was in his mid-50s and tall, more than 6 feet, 4 inches but quite thin, which was not uncommon for cardiologists, who tended to eat healthy, heart-conscious diets. He wore jeans, a white Ralph Lauren shirt, and a blue blazer. He looked comfortable and spoke with a quiet authority.

Smith mentioned that, within the last decade, the Michigan health system had expanded and bought a collection of community hospitals in order to increase its market share, improve buying power from vendors, and ne-gotiate better rates with insurers. The newly amalgamated institution was renamed Michigan Medicine.

The strategy worked financially for Michigan Medicine, but the university doctors were overwhelmingly opposed. Smith told the group that previ-ously, 100 percent of his time was spent at the university hospital. His routine and team were proficient and efficient. Their outcomes and results exceeded the national average for survival and morbidity. But with the expansion, he found himself with inexperienced technicians and nurses. It was not a good situation.

Michael told the group that he had high standards and did not accept mediocrity from his coworkers. His demands and desire for excellence made him unpopular. He was driven and hardworking, so the more laid-back atmosphere of the new community hospital was not conducive to his style. He complained to the nursing director and the chief of cardiology at Michigan Medicine, but they did not commiserate about the issues he raised, and demanded he take his turn in Grand Rapids and Kalamazoo. He had no choice.

One day, he was covering the cath lab in Kalamazoo when a 60-year-old male was brought by ambulance to the emergency department with an obvious heart attack. Michael was paged to the ED, where he told the staff that the patient needed an emergent, immediate catheterization. But when he arrived at the procedure room less than 30 minutes later, the patient hadn't been prepped, even though every second was essential to save the man's life.

Smith went ballistic. He screamed at the nurses, using profanity, before walking out. When paged again, he refused to answer the call. Another less-experienced cardiologist performed the procedure and stent placement. Fortunately, the patient survived, but Michael told the group that his troubles were just beginning.

Smith was placed on probation. The chief of cardiology was furious with him and wanted to fire him on the spot. He wrote personal letters of apology to every member of the emergency department and the cath lab at Kalamazoo Hospital and pleaded with his boss to reinstate him. The thought of having to uproot his family, leave Ann Arbor, and find another job terrified him. Fortunately, with time tempers cooled, and the crisis was averted, but part of the remediation was enrollment in the distressed physicians course. "And that's that."

Andrew, Bruce, and Alan, now coalescing as a unified group, thanked Michael for sharing his story and wished him well.

"Hang in there, buddy," Brian said.

Sugarland suggested the group take a break to stretch their legs.

Andrew pulled out his phone to check his messages. Marissa had texted that she was well. She'd visited the Country Music Hall of Fame and the Ryman Auditorium and had a delicious fried chicken biscuit for lunch at Biscuit Love in the Gulch, a hole-in-the-wall restaurant that was not to be missed. She told Andrew that the shopping in the city proper was pretty honky-tonk and touristy—the better stores were all in the Greenville Mall, a 100-store complex with high-end shops situated between the city and the affluent suburbs, where stars like Garth Brooks, Taylor Swift, Keith Urban, and Nicole Kidman lived.

After a few minutes of catching up, Andrew told her that he had to go. It would be his turn to share next.

When the group reassembled, Guy Worley loaded the next presentation, an introduction to mindfulness. Andrew was relieved to have another lesson before having to relate the details of his ordeal to the group.

Worley began by declaring that mindfulness was the opposite of flooding.

"Mindfulness connects us to the moment, it makes us present. Using mindfulness as a tactic against flooding requires negotiation, listening, and a system of rewards."

He told them that one strategy was to calmly listen first. Talking less and listening more is the reason why we have two ears and one mouth, he joked. Worley's next series of slides demonstrated the practice of mindfulness to emote a calm atmosphere and attitude.

"Whether you're walking or reading, pause to feel your emotions. Find a quiet place, relax, focus your eyes on an object, and concentrate on your breathing."

The men nodded. Andrew felt both bored and anxious.

"Any questions, comments?"

No one raised a hand.

"Dr. Brown, after the lunch break, you're up," Sugarland said.

* * *

"Well, where to begin?" Facing the band of brothers after the break, Andrew explained that he was a New Yorker who'd gone to undergrad at Haverford, medical school at Rutgers, and completed his postgrad training at Johns Hopkins. He told the group that he had been a pediatric oncologist at the University of New York ever since. His career spanned more than 40 years.

Alan Chisholm asked, "Andrew, how did you choose pediatric oncology as a career?"

At Rutgers in the early 1970s, children with cancer were cared for by Arnie Silver, the chief of medical oncology, who had also been Andrew's first mentor. He vividly remembered treating a seven-year-old girl with leukemia. The diagnosis was evident, treatment ineffective chemotherapy with vincristine, prednisone orally and a new drug 6-mercpatopurine for maintenance, the predicted outcome poor, death certain.

tantamount to a death sentence. Fifty years ago, the cure rate for leukemia was less than 10 percent. Brown, however, saw this as an opportunity. He loved caring for children and believed he could enter the field on the ground floor and have an impact on children's lives. He had never looked back.

Brown told the group that he became head of the pediatric oncology division at the University of New York in the mid-1990s, built a first-class, nationally recognized children's cancer program, recruited and mentored more than 15 physicians and scientists, and trained scores of fellows. He had created Hope for Tomorrow, a charity that over the years had raised nearly $100 million to support patient care, education, and research. Brown's philanthropic efforts were used to endow four chairs, and he established a leukemia and lymphoma research laboratory. Brown believed that by every measure he had enjoyed a long, successful career. But he had a heavy temper and was prone to profanity. And for that, he paid a heavy price.

Andrew explained that the specific incident that had resulted in his being placed on an administrative timeout involved an insurance company and his outrage at their failure to allow the transfer of a child newly diagnosed with leukemia to Rose Children's Hospital. He allowed his emotions to turn south, flooding had occurred, rage and profanity rained down.

"My behavior was inappropriate and inexcusable. I know that now." He paused, considering. "Maybe I am...in a way...a distressed physician. I'm glad to be here." He smiled at Sugarland, saying, "I wasn't at first, but I am now."

Sugarland thanked Andrew and told him he recognized how difficult it had been for him to admit he needed help and to accept the course for distressed physicians. "I'm proud of you. You've come a long way."

Shifting gears, Sugarland clapped his hands and said, "All right, boys, next on the agenda is a discussion about harassment in the workplace." Sugarland emphasized the importance of the topic and encouraged them to engage conversation and cross talk.

He told the group that he would present a case study that actually happened at another top-ranked academic medical center. The alleged accused had been a course participant and had granted Sugarland permission to use his story for instruction and constructive purposes, as long as he was not identified.

Clearing his throat, he began.

Dr. X was a powerbroker at an august, prominent institution in the Northeast—top-ranked medical school, top-ranked hospital, a bastion of liberal, progressive thought and practice, a healthcare system that preached diversity, inclusion, and equality. X was the director of pulmonology, a highly regarded National Institutes of Health (NIH)–funded researcher, expert in pulmonary hypertension, extraordinary division chief, recruiter, mentor, and steward of the division finances. He also served as the vice chair for research in the department of medicine and as a member of the executive committee of the faculty practice organization. Dr. X was the whole package, a proven leader who was well-liked by all.

One afternoon, Dr. X received a call from Dr. A, the chair of the department of medicine, requesting his presence immediately in his office. When X arrived at Dr. A's office, seated at the elliptical conference table were Dr. Y, an associate dean of the medical school, and Dr. Z, the chief medical officer of the university hospital.

Without much preamble, Dr. A told X that he was being suspended from the medical staff effective immediately, his hospital and university privileges similarly suspended. Dr. A told him to clear out his office, remove his personal belongings, and leave his university and hospital ID badges and all keys on the desk in his office. Security would escort him out of the building at 6 p.m.

"What's going on?" Dr. X spluttered.

The associate dean handed him an envelope marked "PERSONAL AND CONFIDENTIAL" and told him the enclosed letter would explain the situation. No discussion, no questions. That was all, nothing else need be discussed.

When X returned to his office, there was a security guard waiting by the door, empty boxes piled high. X asked for a minute, retreated inside the office—an office that was distinctly his, with his desk, his chair, his photos, his diplomas, his books, his computer, his papers. He was in a state of shock, his vision blurred and a nauseated quivering in his stomach. He sat at the desk, perhaps for the last time, and opened the letter from the dean of the medical school. The correspondence was terse and direct. He read it several times. Without specifics or detail, the letter indicated that, effective immediately, his rights and privileges as an officer of the university were suspended. It referred X to the hospital bylaws and university faculty handbook. No details were provided, other than a statement that his behavior was abhorrent and unprofessional.

X had become persona non grata. His computer was confiscated, his email account was closed, but no information was made available—nothing, silence. X knew that short of being a convicted felon, the only alleged crime that necessitated such swift, decisive action was an accusation of sexual harassment. But he was at a loss to recall a single incident of inappropriate behavior of any kind. Where had this come from?

He was embarrassed and began to feel out of touch with reality. The conversation with his wife was difficult—impossible, actually. He was not certain she believed him initially. How would he explain the situation to his adult children? Would they judge him? He was hanging on by a thread, and, cut loose, he momentarily considered walking out and leaving the country. Even suicide crossed his mind. He was desperate.

He called Dr. A, someone he'd known and worked with for 25 years…and received no response. He called human resources, Dr. Y, Dr. Z, and the associate dean, and received no response.

He soon discovered that Dr. A had spoken to the members of his division, his friends and colleagues, and instructed them to sever all ties and not to respond to any communication Dr. X sent them.

Fortunately, he had tenure at the university and would continue to receive the base minimum salary allowable. It was hardly sufficient for X and his wife to maintain the lifestyle they had built and grown accustomed to, but at least it was something. They resided in a university-owned apartment and paid below-market rent. He would not vacate the apartment, determining that it might act as a bargaining chip down the road—perhaps if he refused to leave, the university would buy him off.

Soon after everything began, X engaged an employment attorney from a large, prestigious firm. He needed an expert with experience in sexual harassment cases, someone who had contacts at the university hospital and medical school where he had been employed for decades. The lawyer's fee was exorbitant, but X had few options—he needed information and a possible path forward.

Working back channels and contacts, his attorney was able to determine that X had been accused of directing threatening, profane language with sexual innuendo at a female subordinate. X's accuser alleged that he'd prevented her career advancement, dressed her down in a public setting, and humiliated her on more than one occasion. He did not ask for sexual favors in return for opportunity, but the university and hospital had no recourse other than immediate termination. The state licensing board suspended his license to practice medicine. The NIH was instructed to immediately terminate his grant funding and direct the dollars to Dr. A's laboratory instead.

X told his attorney that the accusations were baseless. He admitted he'd had an uncomfortable discussion with his accuser, because she was academically dishonest. But he maintained that under no circumstances had he used inappropriate language or threatened her in any way. The university and hospital endlessly delayed contact. Despite his lawyer's best efforts, filings and demands were denied, and X was refused his proverbial day in court. He attempted to pursue other employment opportunities at other academic centers—all efforts were blocked. No one would hire X or even talk to him. He was an island unto himself.

Sugarland paused and asked the group, "Any thoughts, comments?"

Michael Smith commented that the line of what was appropriate versus inappropriate had narrowed significantly. He said that at Michigan, many male doctors were fearful that any personal comment they might make to female coworkers would be misconstrued, so they limited their conversations to patient care. Smith believed the pendulum had swung too far, but he was in no position to challenge or test it.

Alan Chisholm said that, although he'd not been involved personally, he knew several psychiatry colleagues who had been accused by patients of sexual misconduct. However, a private practice setting is different altogether—allegations are brought to the state medical board, where hearings would occur, and all parties would have an opportunity to present their case.

Guy Worley turned to Andrew. "Dr. Brown, any thoughts?"

"Honestly, the entire situation terrifies me."

Andrew said that listening to Dr. X's experience, he couldn't help but think of his own. The mysterious accusations and days of waiting without any information felt all too familiar. Andrew told the group that he felt relieved that his accuser had complained of anger and language rather than sexual harassment. The boundary was narrow. Brown knew vaguely of two similar situations at the University of New York, though he lacked many details, having heard them secondhand. The first involved a prominent scientist in the molecular genetics department who'd been on the short list for a Nobel Prize until he was fired for propositioning a post-doc in his lab. The second involved a division director in OB/GYN under similar circumstances—here one day, gone the next. No questions asked, no opportunity for explanation or defense.

"Aha!" Sugarland interjected. "Dr. Brown has identified the issue."

He continued, explaining that the difference between an accusation of sexual harassment and one of bad behavior—anger, rage, profanity, regardless of the etiology—was, in many cases, situational. Whereas one might view a situation as an issue of conduct, others might interpret the same event as sexual harassment. The consequences and repercussions were similarly open to interpretation, based on the specific culture and mores of the workplace environment. Some institutions embraced a zero-tolerance approach with swift action and termination, as had happened to Dr. X. Alabama, as was the case with Brian Hamilton, was significantly more tolerant, imposing a stiff reprimand, temporary suspension, attendance at a course for distressed physicians, and reinstatement—embarrassing, but not career-ending.

"What eventually happened to Dr. X?" Bruce Tyler asked.

Sugarland told the group that X's ordeal was long, painful, expensive, and almost ended his career. Although all his privileges were terminated, according to university policy he continued to receive a minimal salary and benefits, including healthcare coverage, as a tenured professor. The hospital reported the incident to the state medical board, and his license to practice medicine was suspended, pending an investigation. The legal action he initiated against the hospital and medical center developed a life of its own, dragging on forever.

The motions and demands of his lawyer were mostly ignored. Dr. X was unable to find another job, either at an academic hospital or in industry. His stellar career in was in ashes; he was tarnished, damaged goods, a pariah. He was despondent, and with his financial resources stretched to the limit, his well did indeed have a bottom. His one saving grace was his family—his wife and children had stuck by his side—otherwise, there was no telling what he might have done.

At long last, after more than two years of letters, judgments, statements, and rulings, his attorney began to make progress. The grounds for reversal of the charges levied against X, and ultimate reinstatement, were predicated on the outcome of a recent similar case. Sugarland reminded the group that he was not a lawyer and understood very little legalese, but that essentially, X's attorney had used the precedent of a United States circuit court that had allowed a lawsuit brought on behalf of a university tennis coach who had been summarily fired for a sexual misconduct complaint by a vindictive female athlete. The coach argued that he was fired because the university was under public pressure to respond to sexual misconduct on campus. The coach, who'd been denied due process, claimed his dismissal constituted sex discrimination and violated federal employment law. The circuit court judge agreed, the coach brought a suit against the university. The case was settled, and he was reinstated, receiving a financial settlement. He left the university, but his character was restored and he was hired as the men's varsity tennis coach at a nationally ranked Pacific Coast conference school.

The outcome of Dr. X's litigation was similar to that of the tennis coach. The state medical board reinstated his license, and he received restitution from the university hospital that had employed him for decades. He could not—would not—return to work as if nothing had transpired. X had nothing to say to Dr. A, not even goodbye. He accepted a position as a faculty member at a university hospital in a different city and state. However, his employment dictated, in part, that he must attend the Carter Singer course for distressed physicians, which he did willingly. Dr. X ultimately felt fortunate to have been given a new life and a second chance.

"What do you think, guys? Should we take a break or call it a day?"

The unanimous consensus was to call it a day. The band of brothers agreed that X's story was emotionally exhausting and terrifying.

"Don't forget the homework assignment in *The Anger Control Workbook*. Tomorrow we will do role playing—the guidelines are in the workbook. See you in the morning."

On the drive back to the to the Hermitage, Andrew was silent and contemplative, choosing to leave the radio off. He left the car with the hotel valet and took the lift to his empty room. Marissa was out and about. He called her cell, and she told him that she was in the lobby and would be up in a few minutes.

That evening, they had an early dinner reservation at Arthur's, a new Nashville iteration from Los Angeles celebrity chef Chas Logan. The restaurant, in a strip mall, lacked Husk's charm, ambience, and excellent cuisine. Andrew was subdued at dinner as he told his wife about the day, reiterating Dr. X's story.

Shaking her head, Marissa said perceptively, "Andrew, you are a lucky dog."

Andrew Brown agreed. He recognized the significance of his transgression, and while he had initially been enraged by its fallout, he now understood that the repercussions could easily have been much worse. His accuser, who remained anonymous to Andrew, could have easily charged him with harassment. The boundary was ill-defined, but the consequences magnified exponentially. Rather than an administrative timeout, which was humiliating and embarrassing for certain, it could have instead resulted in termination, loss of privileges, suspension of his license, loss of income, lawyers, and exorbitant expense.

Holy crap…an entirely different specter of trouble. Yes, indeed. Marissa was right. He was a lucky dog.

CHAPTER 13

DAY THREE IN THE MUSIC CITY

When Andrew's alarm rang the next morning, he was already awake. He lay silently in bed next to Marissa, thinking about his third and final day with the group. Role playing was on the agenda, an exercise he loathed. However, he had committed himself to participating completely and had promised Marissa that he would be a good sport. He rose quietly so as not to disturb her, showering, shaving, and dressing in silence. When he came back into the bedroom, Marissa was awake, propped up in bed and watching CNN.

There was a knock on the door—room service. The server entered the room and opened a small table, upon which he elegantly set up the breakfast offerings. Marissa rose to join Andrew, and they shared perfect oatmeal with raisins, walnuts and brown sugar, and orange juice, with coffee and a scone for Andrew and a bagel with smoked salmon and cream cheese spread for Marissa.

The plan was for Marissa to drop Andrew at Carter Singer and spend another day exploring while he completed his course. In the evening, she would pick him up and they'd drive directly to the airport, where they had a flight booked to Newark that evening. Just one last day to get through.

When Andrew arrived at the lobby of the Clark Office Building, he found Bruce Tyler and Michael Smith chatting.

"Good morning, boys."

The collective mood seemed lighter and less intense than the previous days. The end was in sight. They chatted about the weather, basketball, and the first reports of the new Coronavirus infection in Wuhan, China. There wasn't much information available about the virus other than the fact that it existed. As scientists and doctors, they were always hearing of various outbreaks around the world—nothing new here. The men stood around the coffee station refilling their cups while the breakfast board remained untouched. Apparently, everyone had eaten breakfast at their hotels, a better option than the free offerings from the Carter Singer Hospital kitchen.

Bill Sugarland, Mike Lawrence, and Guy Worley chatted casually with the band of brothers, but before long Sugarland gently ended the conversation.

"Okay," he said. "Let's get started."

Time for the dreaded role play.

One at a time, Bruce Taylor, Brian Hamilton, Michael Smith, Alan Chisholm, and Andrew Brown recreated the episode of bad behavior or potential harassment that had landed them in the group to begin with. Each doctor was tasked with play acting his own role in the incident while the others took on supporting roles. The first three drills went smoothly.

Tyler needed little coaxing to understand that alcoholism is not conducive to a career as a heart surgeon, and that attempting to perform coronary artery bypass surgery or a mitral valve replacement while under the influence put patients at great risk. Brian Hamilton likewise recognized that his treatment of younger female colleagues was despicable and that in a less tolerant environment he could have been stripped of everything he had worked so hard to achieve. Michael Smith's situation was similarly straight-forward—his outburst and temper were inexcusable.

Alan Chisholm's situation was less obvious. The group agreed that, just as patients have the ability to select their doctors, physicians should have the ability to discharge patients from their care if the chemistry and bond between them is a failure. During his role-play exercise, Alan demonstrated a calm patience. He explained that he no longer believed he could be of value to the patient. He had stated unequivocally that the patient deserved better from their doctor and Alan indicated he could no longer provide care. Alan offered the patient a list of three psychiatrists as options, but the patient refused his advice and demonstrated outrage. With anger and rancor, the patient said, "You can't fire me! You're an asshole! You'll never get away with this!"

Alan had tried desperately to find another psychiatrist for his recalcitrant patient, to no avail. Nevertheless, he was made the responsible party for the outcome of a tragic situation. What alternative did he really have? He had tried. Alan asked the group, "Was I to blame for the death of my former patient?"

The room was silent. The band of brothers had no answer. It was a terrible situation with no winners, only losers.

In Andrew's situation, however, everyone in the group recognized that the incident had been cut and dried, his behavior abhorrent. Therefore, he asked to role play a different scenario that he encountered often, a scenario that involved a systems failure at the University of New York.

He explained to the group that high-dose methotrexate is an effective chemotherapy treatment for lymphoblastic leukemia as well as osteosarcoma, a malignant bone tumor. At Rose Children's Hospital, patients might receive the drug as a prolonged infusion for 8 to 24 hours, followed by hydration and leucovorin rescue. The day of admission, the children arrive in the clinic for intravenous fluids and wait for an inpatient bed to become available. More often than not, the kids spend the entire day in the outpatient area, arrive at the inpatient unit late in the afternoon or early evening during a nursing shift change or resident sign-out, and the methotrexate infusion doesn't begin until the middle of the night. The system was unsafe and inefficient, adding an entire day to the length of the hospital stay, increasing the cost of care. The predicament was a frustration and disappointment to staff, physicians, nurses, patients, and families alike.

Andrew told the group that he had complained about the system vociferously and frequently to anyone who would listen. It was a constant irritant and trigger for his anger and temper. The issue was that the hospital pharmacy, billing, and compliance were unwilling or unable to merge an outpatient charge with an inpatient charge. They had separate and antiquated systems, and the patients were left to suffer. Other institutions had solved the problem, why not the University of New York?

As he explained his frustrations to the group, Andrew became agitated. Just thinking about the failures of the system made his blood boil. Everyone implored Andrew to give it a rest.

Sit on the wall, close your eyes, and take deep breaths.

Guy Worley noted that Andrew's persistent annoyance and reaction to an issue about which he had no input or control was the definition of insanity: "Repeating an action over and over and expecting a different result." The group agreed unanimously with Worley's conclusion.

The men took a coffee break, and when they resumed, the conversation was informal. Sugarland, Worley, Mike Lawrence, and Beth White reviewed and summarized salient points from previous sessions, focusing on the concept of "flooding," reiterating strategies to terminate a rapid escalation of emotions and downward spiral into the abyss of anger, temper, and rage. A key tactic, they said, was to be able to see the issue from both sides. Take a breath, sit on the wall, and step outside the intensity of the moment long enough to consider the opposing perspective.

"In most cases, who is right and who is wrong lies in the middle—in that elusive common ground," said Sugarland. "In order to get there, you need to communicate effectively. You need to speak with respect, honesty, and specificity."

He went to the board and wrote out: DRAN—describe, reinforce, assert, negotiate.

"In context," he explained, "The D, or 'describe,' refers to one's ability to define another person's behavior or actions themselves, rather than their motives or what you perceive as the results of their action. The more specifics you apply to the concept—like time, place, and frequency—the better. Reinforce the positive aspects, respect the rights of others, and be assertive without demonstrating aggression. Remember that solutions are best reached through compromise. The act of being assertive does not necessitate an unyielding single-mindedness—just the opposite, in fact."

Worley told the group to listen first, gathering information to formulate a thoughtful response. He emphasized that the ability to express an opinion calmly and thoughtfully is a powerful tool that indicates self-control and a willingness to solve problems.

"Calm patience is more powerful than anger."

Sugarland asked the group if anyone had any questions or comments. Hearing none, he told the group that the tradition was to have a special last meal to celebrate the group's hard work. Lunch would be prepared and delivered by Charlie's Famous, a landmark Nashville restaurant that served traditional Southern barbecue—fried chicken, barbecued ribs, pulled pork, collard greens, sweet potatoes, hush puppies, and pecan pie for dessert. Beer, wine, iced tea, and lemonade would also be provided.

Lunch was a welcome treat. The decadent food helped the men to relax. They spoke easily with the staff about the upcoming NFL playoffs and how, miraculously, the Tennessee Titans had remained in play. They agreed that their next opponent, the Kansas City Chiefs, and their brilliant quarterback, Skip Magor, would be a formidable challenge.

Noticeably, there was one topic that everyone wanted to avoid: Donald Trump. His presidency, social media presence, actions, comments, policies (or lack thereof)—everything about him was polarizing. Either you loved or loathed him, and the safest course of action in an environment of relative strangers was avoidance. Political discussions had the potential to trigger adverse comments or incite a display of temper, both of which were contrary to the lessons the men had learned over the past few days. They had been taught that avoidance was the first and most important reaction to a noxious stimulus, and Trump was a noxious stimulus, no matter how you sliced it.

Rising from his seat and wiping his mouth with a napkin, Sugarland told the group how much he had enjoyed meeting each of them. He noted that the diversity of the attendees with respect to geography and specialty had been a particular strength, and that he and the other staff—Guy Worley, Mike Lawrence, and Beth White—all agreed that this group had been particularly gratifying to work with. Sugarland reminded the group to practice the lessons they had learned—mindfulness, avoidance, calm.

"Keep your course binder and *The Anger Control Workbook* as a reference," he told them. He wrote his email address and mobile phone number on the whiteboard and encouraged the participants to contact him directly with questions and concerns.

"Alrighty then…that's a wrap!"

Bruce Tyler, Brian Hamilton, Alan Chisholm, Michael Smith, and Andrew Brown all stood, passing handshakes around. Andrew felt relieved. He was happy to be done and eager to get back to New York, but he had to admit that it hadn't been nearly as painful as he had thought it would be. Was it worth the outrageous price tag? No. Could he have achieved similar results with Ginnie Parvich? Likely. But still, there was something reassuring about meeting the other men who, despite illustrious careers and accolades, had struggled similarly. Though he doubted it would happen, Andrew sincerely hoped they would all stay in touch.

Marissa arrived early and was waiting in front of the building when Andrew exited. She smiled and greeted him with a hug. "Hi, honey. I'm proud of you for sticking with it. Really, I am. I hope you learned something here and take it with you."

Before he could answer, Andrew's mobile phone beeped. There was a message from United Airlines saying that their flight to Newark had been delayed a couple hours because of bad weather in the New York area.

He smiled at Marissa and shrugged. "Oh well, what can you do?"

Her shoulders relaxed. "Wow," she said, beaming. "I guess you really did learn something!"

Marissa suggested that since they had a couple extra hours to kill, they visit the Hillsboro Village neighborhood of Nashville. The guidebook said that there were galleries, shops, and the Belmont Mansion, a sprawling summer estate built between 1849 and 1860 by the wealthiest female slave owner in America. The mansion was spectacular, and the grounds magnificent with gardens, riding stables, and a zoo. After a short visit to the mansion, a gift shop sojourn, and a latte at the cafe, Andrew and Marissa drove to the airport, returned the rental car, and settled in with their respective laptops to wait for their flight home, now delayed an additional two hours.

CHAPTER 14

TRIUMPHANT RETURN TO UNY

On Monday morning, Andrew called Jeff Flack's office and asked his assistant Anna Valencia when he could see his boss. Anna told him that Dr. Flack was expecting his call and had time to talk Tuesday morning at 10 o'clock.

Next, Andrew emailed Ginnie Parvich to make an appointment and share the experiences of his week. She was interested in the details of the course, as she and her colleagues in psychiatry at the University of New York had discussed instituting a similar—albeit shorter—program, dedicated to physicians and key staff at UNY Hospital and Medical Center. Anger, bad behavior, and harassment were relatively common among high-level professionals, not only in medicine, but in law offices, financial service firms, and across corporate America. Not a surprise.

The university and hospital mandated that all faculty and staff complete an annual online sexual harassment training course. The focus was on improper conduct with respect to relationships, solicitation, language, hostility, and obscene gestures with sexual innuendo in the workplace. However, the training did not address the wide spectrum of harassment and potential career suppression between faculty with oversight and their direct reports. If Andrew Brown had learned one takeaway message from his time at Carter Singer, it was that the boundary between harassment and displays of temper was narrow at best. It was deeply subjective, and everything could be on the line.

On Tuesday morning, Jeff Flack greeted Andrew warmly, ushered him into his office, and thanked him for attending the course. Flack peppered Andrew with questions about the other participants, the incidents that had led them to attend, where they came from, and the course's overall value.

Andrew told Jeff that there had been five physicians in attendance, all men, and that four of the five were from major academic medical schools. One by one, Andrew described each member of the band of brothers, their backstories, and their experiences during the course.

"And then there was me." Andrew explained that he appreciated that the Carter Singer course was part of the reinstatement and remediation process. No one attended voluntarily, but everyone in his group wound up leaving with the impression that the course had been of value for their personal growth.

"It was a grounding, humbling experience. I know I was vehemently opposed to attending at first, but I'm really glad I went." The course was intense, the instructors were extremely knowledgeable, and the other physicians' experiences had taught Andrew a lot about his own.

The experience had been immersive, the readings instructive and informative, and the homework assignments complementary. All this culminated in him being forced to concentrate and confront the root cause of his anger.

"How would you compare what you gleaned from the course to your sessions with Ginnie Parvich?"

Andrew replied that, although the ultimate endpoint may have been similar, the acquisition of skills to prevent and mitigate anger and rage in the group setting was significantly more durable. The intent of both the course and individual therapy was behavior modification—however, the group dynamic had proved to be a powerful reinforcement he had not appreciated during individual treatment.

With that being said, Andrew added that he believed every situation and occurrence had value. He told Flack that he and Dr. Parvich, with the assistance of Stergios Dimutri, a neurobiologist, were researching a possible anger gene and the hereditary nature of anger and rage.

Flack seemed pleased, even impressed, by the enthusiasm with which Andrew was approaching this challenge. "This all sounds good, Andrew," he said. "I commend you for your flexibility, for attending the course, and for your desire to learn."

The men shook hands. "Before you leave," Flack said. "I have one last question." He smiled. "How did you like Nashville?"

"Honestly? Not very much," Andrew admitted, laughing. "Country music isn't my thing...I'm a New Yorker."

Wednesday afternoon was a bitterly cold New York winter day. Rather than don his coat, hat, and gloves, Andrew took the indoor route. When he exited the elevator, Dr. Parvich was already standing at the reception desk speaking with the registrar. She turned and extended her hand in greeting.

"Welcome home."

"Great to be back."

Andrew followed Ginnie into her office, and they took their usual seats facing one another.

"So, how was it? Tell me everything."

Andrew told Ginnie that the course had been a worthwhile experience. The instructors were knowledgeable, professional, collegial. The curriculum was focused on guiding the participants on their path forward and helping them to recognize bad behavior, prevent flooding, and avoid inappropriate outbursts. He reminded Ginnie how vehemently opposed he had been to attending the course at Carter Singer, convinced he had nothing to learn there that their sessions together wouldn't cover more sufficiently.

"But Ginnie, I was wrong. You have been wonderful, and you've provided a foundation that has allowed me to be more receptive," he said, not wanting to give her the wrong idea. "But the course really cemented all that I had previously learned from our sessions. It brought a lot of things together for me and, most importantly, prepared me to execute my new skills."

Ginnie asked about the other participants, their transgressions, and where they were from. Andrew briefly explained that the band of brothers were men in mid-career, except one outlier, the psychiatrist from Ohio. He continued to enumerate the varied offenses that necessitated their participation, including verbal abuse, harassment, and alcoholism, as well as temper. He mentioned that he recognized similarities in the trials and tribulations—bad behavior being the common denominator—among all the participants, himself included.

Though he left him unnamed, Andrew told Ginnie that Alan Chisholm's situation continued to haunt him—it had seemed the most troubling to everyone.

It was unsettling. A life was lost, but did Alan really contribute to the death of the patient? Was there a direct correlation between the patient's discharge and his suicide? Should Chisholm have recognized that the patient was capable of taking his own life? Should he have reported his concerns to the patient's family, the authorities, a suicide help line? Where did the boundaries between doctor and patient lie? With so many unanswered questions and such subjectivity, Andrew worried for his own future. Obviously, the state of Ohio had reinstated Chisholm and permitted him to continue his practice, but that was, of course, far from the end of the ordeal.

Continuing, Andrew told Ginnie that there had been a session on family history, the results of which had implied that anger may in fact be hereditary—a confirmation of the research that they had discussed with Stergios. Perhaps the presence of an anger gene was real. But, regardless of etiology, the therapeutic management involved behavior modification. Andrew told Ginnie that he had asked Sugarland and other staff members if they were familiar with the concept of an inherited anger gene, monoamine oxidase-A dysfunction, or dysregulation. Sugarland had read something about hereditary anger genes but was far from an expert on the subject. He indicated the intent of the family history exercise was to demonstrate that anger, rage, and bad behavior often seemed to run in families, particularly among the men. Whether this implied a genetic contribution or an abnormal gene remained to be seen.

"That all sounds very positive, Andrew. And how has your homework been? Were there any inciting incidents that gave you an opportunity to practice the mitigating strategies we discussed?"

Andrew told Ginnie about his delayed flight and a few other minor annoyances that might have once infuriated him. "But I was able to keep a cool head about it! You know, it's funny. When I'm able to avoid flooding, I can actually take a step back and see how silly and meaningless these things are."

Ginnie beamed at him proudly.

Andrew reminded Ginnie that their research work was not complete. "I really would like to invite you and Stergios to Rhinebeck to enjoy the Hudson Valley and continue our conversation."

"I think that's a great idea! I enjoy Dr. Dimutri's company, and I think he'll be very helpful to our project," Ginnie said. "And like I said, I've never been to the Hudson River Valley."

"Well, we'll make it happen! Rhinebeck in the spring is a special place."

Later that day, Andrew received emails from Barry Steinglass and Dean Smith indicating that they understood from Jeff Flack that the Nashville course had been a success. Both thanked him for attending and welcomed him home.

Andrew Brown's stock was rising. In some odd way, he felt that he commanded new respect and admiration. A good thing for sure!

CHAPTER 15

RHINEBECK

Spring in Rhinebeck is a season for renewal. Winters in the Hudson Valley can be long and harsh, with snowbanks covering the ground well into April. However, once the daffodils and crocuses break through the ice, the flowering Japanese dogwoods, cherry blossoms, peonies, and *Astilbes* are soon to arrive.

The snow had melted, and spring was in full bloom when Andrew Brown sent an email to Ginnie Parvich and Stergios Dimutri inviting them to spend a weekend, or at least a Saturday, in Rhinebeck. He suggested a weekend in mid-May and told them that they were welcome to bring their spouses and children if they'd like.

Ginnie and Stergios confirmed their availability. Ginnie would bring her husband, Lawrence Shine, and Stergios his wife, Liani. They agreed that leaving their children at home with grandparents would make for a more relaxing weekend away, though they politely declined Andrew's offer to spend the night at his home. They would instead stay at the Beekman Arms Inn, a historic hotel and town anchor located in the center of Rhinebeck's historic district. The Inn was one of America's oldest continuously operated hotels—during the Revolutionary War, it had hosted the likes of George Washington, Benedict Arnold, and Alexander Hamilton. Given the nature of their shared project, the history and gravitas of the place felt like a natural fit.

The trio's lunch at Local felt like a distant memory to Andrew, and Nashville was similarly in the rearview mirror. Thoughts of anger, on the other hand, were never far from his mind. He had launched himself fully into the question of whether temper had any positive aspects—any outcomes of value. He read voraciously, and to his surprise, found that extensive information existed on the subject. He took copious notes and was excited to share his research with Ginnie and Stergios during their visit.

Rhinebeck was about 90 miles due north of the city, and the Browns' nine-room, 19th-century barn-style dwelling was just a short 2-mile drive from the village. Marissa and Andrew had renovated virtually the entire interior—kitchen, bathrooms, sunroom, screen porch, and entry foyer—while retaining the exterior's historic charm. Marissa had exquisite taste. Her furnishings and artwork were cultivated, comfortable, and functional. There was a stream and waterfall on their 3-acre property replete with small brook trout. The sound of rushing water careening off the rocks added a sense of natural calm.

Marissa planted and enjoyed a bountiful vegetable garden. In late summer, her six raised beds yielded a bumper crop of tomatoes, onions, zucchini, cucumbers, and a multitude of herbs and spices. Andrew's passion, the perennial plantings, formed a colorful mosaic in constant bloom from spring to fall.

The Saturday morning of Ginnie's and Stergios's visit dawned beautiful and cloudless, the sun radiant and warm. Andrew and Marissa were up early to prepare lunch for their guests, who were expected at noon. Marissa suggested an antipasto of cheese, charcuterie, olives, and roasted red peppers, a fresh-baked baguette, a vegetable lasagna, a white Sancerre, and biscotti with coffee. Andrew agreed heartily.

Marissa handed Andrew a shopping list with three stops: the Village Wine Shop for the Sancerre; Bread Alone for freshly baked baguettes, biscotti, and freshly made ricotta cannoli (not on the list, but irresistible); and Carlo and Oscar's Market for olives, peppers, Parmigiano-Reggiano, Manchego,

Pecorino Romano, pepperoni, spicy salami, prosciutto, fresh heirloom to-matoes, and sundried tomatoes in olive oil. Beyond delicious.

The vegetable lasagna of spinach, butternut squash, and ricotta was assem-bled and ready for the oven when Andrew returned. He placed the pack-ages on the center counter, then put the wine in the cooler and the other perishables in the refrigerator.

"Should I set the table in the sunroom?" he asked.

The sunroom, open to the kitchen, had two skylights and floor-to-ceil-ing windows overlooking the stream, ornamental grasses, and hundreds of ferns of the back property. On the left side of the room was a glass-topped wrought-iron table with six matching chairs. Andrew placed six plates, sil-verware, crystal stemware, and cloth napkins on the table, but something was missing.

"We really should have fresh-cut flowers as a centerpiece," Andrew said. He headed back to the market for something colorful after seeing their own garden barely beginning to bloom. He purchased an arrangement of pink, purple, and white lilies, peonies, roses, baby's breath, and greens.

Ginnie and Lawrence were the first to arrive. Andrew and Marissa greeted them and welcomed them to the Hudson Valley. Ginnie told Marissa that although they had not met previously, she felt as if she knew her well.

Marissa said, "I know what you mean. I feel similarly."

Dr. Shine extended his hand to Andrew and Marissa. "Thank you so much for inviting us to your home. Rhinebeck is a lovely little town. It's easy to see why you've made it your home."

Before long, a new teal BMW 530i xDrive turned onto Ridge Road, head-lights flashing. Stergios and Liani Dimutri had arrived. Andrew walked to the car. "Welcome—perfect timing!"

Stergios said the ride had been easy and quite pleasant. Introductions were made all around. Everyone was in a good mood, pleased to be together in the country and looking forward to a relaxing two-day respite, far removed from the city. Marissa performed a walkthrough tour of the house. There were rave reviews all around. Andrew watched with pride. He loved his house—it was beyond terrific. It was the right size, and everything about it was tastefully put together with thought and care. Marissa's influence was evident in every room. After the tour everyone gathered in the kitchen.

Liani Dimutri commented about the three paintings in the living room. "They seem to be of similar style—did the same artist paint all three? They're quite interesting. I love the technique."

Marissa told the group that her father, a bona fide artist, had painted all three pieces as well as the large canvas in the foyer.

"As a teenager, my father designed the Fiorello La Guardia medallion for the 1939 World's Fair in New York City," she said, beaming with pride. "He founded a full-service advertising agency, Stein Shapiro, and served as the art director of the firm. Eventually, he sold his share of the business to his partners and devoted his efforts to creating art. My parents were urban pioneers; they bought a 5,000-square-foot loft on West Broadway in the late 1960s that served as their studio and living space. It was very cool and very ahead of the times. Some of my father's work was truly extraordinary. The pieces Andrew and I have are among our personal favorites. He was particularly skilled at painting the human form and countenance. If you look closely at the painting in the living room on the far wall, you can see my mother and me as subjects."

Making her way to the counter, Marissa told the group that lunch was a buffet. She placed the bubbling hot vegetable lasagna on a trivet on the center island, with the cheese and charcuterie platter, baguettes, butter, and Sancerre on either side of the main event. Everyone served themselves, poured a glass of wine, and sat at the table in the adjacent sunroom. The food was exquisite, the conversation light. Weather, children, and summer plans were all touched upon—there was no mention of anger, temper, or rage.

Andrew raised a glass, "To my colleagues and friends, thank you for joining us today, and thank you for your time and expertise. Ginnie, Stergios—you have taught me much, and I am grateful."

"Hear! Hear!"

At the conclusion of the repast, Ginnie and Liani stood to help clear the table while the men remained seated.

Marissa asked, "Would anyone care for coffee or tea with dessert?"

Andrew went to the refrigerator and removed the pièce de résistance. He arranged the plain ricotta, chocolate, and salted caramel cannoli on a plate, placing the biscotti on a second plate. After lunch, Andrew told his guests that in the Brown household there was a standing rule that there could be no discussion about the next meal until the previous one was completed.

"Therefore, let me tell you about dinner," he said, his guests laughing appreciatively. He told them that they had a reservation at the Beekman Arms at 7:30 that evening. "Convenient, for sure."

Ginnie Parvich and Stergios understood that a continued discussion of their research on anger was on the agenda for the afternoon. Lawrence asked if he could participate as well, and the others agreed—his perspective could provide a useful outsider's point of view.

Marissa invited Liani to do some antiquing—the number of shops in the area was too many to count. As the two drove off in Liani's BMW, Marissa asked her about her childhood.

Liani told Marissa that she had been born in Tehran in 1982 during the Iran-Iraq War. "We lived in the northern part of the city, in a region called

Naft. It was a beautiful, affluent region with parks, town squares, wonderful schools, and shopping. My father, an economist educated at Oxford, was also a financier and worked for the Central Bank of Iran and as an advisor to Mohammad Reza Pahlavi, the Shah of Iran."

In 1979, the Shah's government collapsed, and he and his family fled into exile in Egypt. The Ayatollah Khomeni, a religious leader, became the supreme leader, and Islamic law was enforced across the country. The Ayatollah denounced the United States, which led to militant Islamic fundamentalist students storming the U.S. Embassy in Tehran in 1979, an occupation that lasted more than a year.

"Our family—my father, mother, and my brother and I—were persecuted and terrorized by the military and secret police loyal to Khomeni. They confiscated our belongings and harassed us day and night. I was unable to attend school. Life was terrible. Each new day brought new fears and dangers. My grandfather was incarcerated and sentenced to be executed for treason when he miraculously escaped, emigrated to California, and became a U.S. citizen."

In September 1980, after a territorial dispute over the Shatt al-Arab waterway, Iraq launched a surprise invasion of Iran. Living in Tehran became untenable for Liani and her family. The threat of invasion was constant, there was no food or water, children were starving, and death and destruction reigned. The war lasted eight years, and while a million people were killed, neither side achieved their goal of toppling the other's regime. There were no winners, only losers, and both countries were left devastated for a generation.

"During the war, my father managed to send my mother, brother, and me to London, but he was not permitted to leave Iran. His passport was confiscated. We spent three years in England without a word from my father—we did not know if he was alive or dead." Her voice trailed off as the emotions and memories welled in her.

Marissa was on the edge of her seat and grateful that Liani had driven so that she could listen attentively. "But your father survived, didn't he? How did he finally get to London?"

"When the war ended, the Islamist government temporarily lost its rigid grip on the population. As a family, we considered returning to Tehran. After all, it was our home. But ultimately, we decided that with so much uncertainty, there was no way of knowing if it would ever be safe to return. My father was able to have his passport reinstated and received a visa to travel to the United Kingdom. After being separated for four years, he joined us in London.

"We had a charming flat in the Saint John's Wood section of the city. We were reunited at last. Our entire family became British citizens. I went to King's College, became a dentist, met Stergios in a pub, got married, had two daughters—Malia and Adelaide—and we came to New York because we both had tremendous job opportunities. We really enjoy living in Rye—the girls are happy, and Stergios and I both have good positions at the University."

Marissa moved closer to Liani and wrapped an arm around her shoulders. "I'm really glad to meet you. You're an incredible woman."

CHAPTER 16

PROS AND CONS

Andrew suggested that they sit on the screen porch to enjoy the warm May breeze as they talked. The sound of cascading water from the stream provided a soothing background lull. There were a wicker sofa, two adjacent wicker chairs, and a glass table intended for the extension of weary legs. Andrew placed his laptop, manila folder, a pitcher of iced tea, and four glasses on the glass-topped table, and took a seat in one of the wicker chairs, leaving the other and the wicker sofa available to his peers.

Leaning back into the deep cushion, he took a deep breath, folded his arms across his chest, and proclaimed, "Anger is good!"

In unison, Stergios and Ginnie said, "Do tell."

Andrew told his guests that since they had last met, he had been intellectually preoccupied with anger—its history from the beginning of recorded time, the possible existence of an anger gene, and the potential positive attributes of anger.

"Anger, like happiness, sadness, or fear, is a primary human emotion. Its intensity may vary from mild irritation to out-of-control rage, but the fact remains: At its most basic level, anger indicates that something is wrong. There is always a *reason* for it. So there's one positive, at least."

Ginnie did not look entirely convinced. "I don't know...do you really think anger is good for the human spirit and condition?" She suggested he recall his past personal experiences with anger. "I don't know there is anything positive there…" She looked hesitant, not wanting to offend.

"There wasn't anything positive!" Andrew replied, unfazed. "That's the problem."

He told his friends and colleagues that in his own past experiences, anger operated like a cancer, multiplying and growing uncontrollably before ultimately destroying everything in its wake.

"And yet, the more I researched, the more evidence I found to the contrary. It *does* have some positive attributes. There's literature claiming that man needs anger to survive—it's part of our body's natural response to provide protection. Without anger, we may be left vulnerable."

Andrew opened his folder and read a quote from Aristotle: "The angry man is aiming at what he can attain, and the belief that you will attain your aim is pleasant."

"I wonder," Lawrence interjected intuitively, "whether a denial of anger may be rooted in social mores. Certainly, some cultures—the Italian culture for instance—allow for the open, and what we would perceive as excessive, expression of anger."

"That's a good point." Ginnie nodded at her husband. "In American culture, men are encouraged to suppress emotions that would indicate sensitivity—like sadness, anxiety, fear—which can then manifest as anger, which is a relatively acceptable emotional expression. Perhaps the issue isn't anger so much as its broader self-expression and the limitations of that self-expression."

The group continued to discuss and dissect this idea, ultimately agreeing that mild to moderate anger may have some positive aspects. They likewise agreed that extreme or chronic rage was undoubtedly detrimental.

Not surprisingly, Stergios was familiar with the concept of constructive temper and rage. "Anger," he said, "is not solely an aggressive reaction but may also provide information that allows improved engagement with the outside world." He asked to borrow Andrew's laptop and searched "Pros and cons of anger."

Everyone was surprised by the plethora of material on the subject. As they scrolled through, one title immediately caught their collective attention—a list of 16 beneficial attributes of anger, complete with references.

"Well," Lawrence said. "If it's in print, it must be true."

The premise of the article was that anger makes humans more informed, as anger is a primitive emotion designed to promote survival. It was an innate response, pushing you to fight back and spontaneously react if threatened. It stimulated emotional and physical pain and encouraged control—a sense of being in charge rather than helpless.

"That all makes sense to me," Andrew said. "My issues with anger are definitely about the loss of control."

Power and influence, the article explained, were often at the root of anger—a "my way or the highway" mentality.

Ginnie nodded. "In my practice, I have not encountered a situation where the need for control suppressed bad behavior."

"Not to mention the health implications," Andrew added. "Temper and violence are associated with adverse, harmful physiological effects. Stress-related illness is real and linked to out-of-control anger. Anger can literally make you sick. Violent, out-of-control anger promotes the release of the stress hormones cortisol, norepinephrine, and adrenaline into the bloodstream, which, in turn, can cause increased heart rate, higher blood pressure, and the formation of blood clots. These risks are greatest within two hours of an outburst and increase the risk of angina, arrhythmias, heart attack, and stroke."

Lawrence Shine questioned if beta blockers—medicines that decrease the heart rate and lower blood pressure—might be used to alleviate anger's toxic effect.

Ginnie and Stergios recalled discussions about the use of antidepressant drugs, specifically selective serotonin reuptake inhibitors (SSRIs) to provide a calm milieu and reduce uncontrollable outbursts in the presence of the possible anger gene, monoamine oxidase-A dysfunction, and the inability to control serotonin levels. All surmised that, while fascinating, their conjectures remained unproven.

Stergios returned to the computer. The next positive attribute listed in the article asserted that, if properly applied, anger could be a bargaining tool. "Anger strongly asserts a position and demands compliance. Anger communicates a message that constructive cooperation is required to resolve conflict."

Ginnie and Lawrence exchanged glances. Anger as a negotiation tactic, they agreed, was just wrong, unacceptable under any circumstances. Ginnie had practical experience in dispute resolution and said that productive conversations had no place for temper. In fact, she indicated that the opposite was far more effective in her world. "Listening calmly, communicating, and attempting to understand the opposing party yields superior results every time," she said.

Andrew shared some of his experiences during the Nashville course that mirrored Ginnie's perspective. His three days of instruction had been clear and simple: be calm and nonconfrontational, walk away, and avoid flooding.

Temper and rage, they agreed, were volcanic emotions, and it behooved an angry individual to investigate the source, address it, and strive for change. In that context, an angry individual committed to change was able to overcome faults and shortcomings, leading to self-improvement, greater emotional intelligence, and renewal.

The crucial takeaway was not to abandon anger as a whole but to react appropriately and situationally. They agreed that there were some benefits to appropriate, controlled anger in helping to assert boundaries. However, if that anger spiraled out of control beyond the initial reaction, it could not lead to productive communication, instead metastasizing into something dangerous and violently destructive.

Stergios recalled a quote from Aristotle that in essence stated that although difficult to achieve, appropriate anger has a place in society.

Andrew told his colleagues and new friends that he was familiar with Aristotle quote. And it resonated with him—in fact, the leaders of the distressed physicians course at Carter Singer in Nashville used the citation to illustrate the difficulty in appropriate anger management.

Just as they concluded the report, Marissa and Liani returned from their antiquing. They didn't have much to show for the effort. Marissa was empty-handed, while Liani had found a blue Roseville vase and matching bowl.

When Marissa asked how their afternoon had been, the group agreed that it had been productive.

Everyone stood and stretched. It was almost 4:30. Andrew reminded his guests that dinner at the Beekman Arms would be at 7:30.

"Marissa and I will meet you in the bar at 7 o'clock for a drink," he said. "See you in a few hours. Dress is casual."

The guests took their leave, and Andrew and Marissa settled in on the couch in the living room to rest up before the evening's socializing. Andrew regurgitated to Marissa as much of the afternoon as he could recall, assuring her that Stergios's and Ginnie's input had been useful. Suddenly overcome with exhaustion, he stretched out on the couch, his legs across Marissa's lap.

"I'm glad you're doing this," she said, giving his foot a reassuring squeeze.

Andrew fell into a light, peaceful sleep.

* * *

The Beekman Arms was charmingly historic but with modern updates. The Colonial Tap Room, adjacent to the main dining room, featured four 200-year-old beams overhead, an oak-paneled bar, and an open hearth, replete with a roaring fire, which was welcome on the cool spring evening.

Everyone arrived on time. Greetings were shared and drinks ordered. The group was relaxed and comfortable. They made pleasant small talk, savoring their drinks until their table in the main dining room was ready.

The farm-to-table menu was typical of the Hudson Valley. Everyone ordered a salad—Caesar, iceberg wedge with bacon lardons, or arugula. Marissa, Liani, and Ginnie all selected the salmon en croûte. The men ordered ribeye steaks and pork chops. Over a local Cabernet, the group enjoyed a light conversation about children, summer plans, and travel. Stergios and Liani were planning a trip to Greece to visit family and friends, a yearly pilgrimage. The girls enjoyed spending time with Stergios's parents on the farm in Larisa, milking cows, fishing, and of course, savoring grandma's heavenly moussaka.

Ginnie's daughter was headed to Belvoir Terrace, a girls' summer camp in the Berkshires, which placed great emphasis on music and the arts. Marissa told everyone that she and Andrew were looking forward to an active summer with friends and family in Rhinebeck. Andrew, always busy, would play golf, fish, garden, and read, while Marissa would visit the local farmers' markets, tend to her vegetable garden, and cook for the family. They would both, of course, spend as much time as possible with their grandchildren, Will and Clara.

After dinner, the conversation continued, even as the restaurant emptied of other patrons and the waitstaff grew eager to clear the table and go home.

As they left the restaurant, Andrew felt a renewed sense of energy and purpose. The day's conversation had been enlightening, and he looked forward to continuing it the following day.

Stergios and Lawrence insisted on paying the bill.

"Thank you, but not necessary," Andrew said. "May I suggest you all have a leisurely morning and come to the house for brunch around 11?"

CHAPTER 17

SUNDAY BRUNCH

Robins and blue jays sang in the courtyard trees, the perfect soundtrack to a beautiful sunlit Sunday morning. While Stergios, Liani, and the Parvich-Shines did a little sightseeing on Market Street, Marissa and Andrew prepared a brunch of challah French toast sprinkled with confectioner's sugar, served with bacon, fresh fruit, and fresh-brewed coffee. They set the sunroom table set for six.

The Sunday edition of *The New York Times* sat on the foyer table, its headlines relaying Trump's latest atrocities. Noticing the paper, Lawrence shook his head with disgust. Andrew and Marissa were relieved to know that their guests shared their distaste for the man, though they were less than eager to open that can of worms. They tried desperately to steer the conversation to another less depressing topic, but to no avail. Thankfully, there was no ranting or raving, merely a calm dialogue of disbelief.

"That's why science and mathematics are so appealing," Stergios said. "It is precise. Answers are forthcoming, apparent. No 'fake news' and 'truthiness.'"

After brunch, everyone retired to the porch for a second cup of coffee. Andrew thanked his guests for making the drive to Rhinebeck, for dinner at the Beekman Arms, and for genuinely helping him to better understand himself and the intricacies of anger. He told Stergios and Ginnie that there was more to learn and that he would continue to read, take notes, and reach out to them in the future to continue their dialogue.

With that, the Shines and the Dimutris were ready to depart. Waving goodbye, Andrew gave Marissa a hug. "Thanks, honey."

"My pleasure. They're all really nice people. I'm glad you connected with them."

Together, they cleared the sunroom table, rinsed the dishes, and loaded the dishwasher. Marissa asked if they could spend the night and drive home in the morning, and Andrew readily agreed.

Though he would normally read for pleasure before bed, Andrew instead settled in behind his computer. He recalled the uncomfortable examples he had revealed to Ginnie Parvich—the out-of-control flooding and anger directed against his defenseless children. He was a bully, plain and simple. The genesis of his behavior was multifactorial. It may even have resided in an anger gene, an inherited trait from his father, but environment and culture most assuredly contributed.

Despite having a multitude of negative consequences, anger, like depression, grief, anxiety, and other powerful emotions, had some appeal. There was some undeniable power in anger. Andrew recognized that there was a middle position, a compromise. But it was the path to the middle that troubled him. He ardently believed that calm reason, respect, and honest discussion was the way.

CHAPTER 18

HISTORY OF ANGER

Andrew Brown sat behind the desk of his office at the University of New York, idly twirling a pen between his fingers and looking out the window at Hamilton Avenue. Below, Andrew watched the midday throng on the crowded sidewalk undulating in and around the University of New York Hospital. He watched men in suits, doctors in white coats, and nurses in blue scrubs. He watched patients, many accompanied by family members, prepare for their visits, procedures, and scans. He watched visitors, taxi and livery drivers, and a multitude of service personnel jostling for space at the main entrance of the hospital building.

Catching himself, Andrew returned his attention to the task before him. The view on Hamilton Avenue was a brief distraction, but Andrew had work to do. He was committed to self-education and learning about all aspects of anger and rage, its history, origins, genetics, and positive and negative effects.

Ginnie Parvich and Stergios Dimutri had been invaluable colleagues. Despite his initial reticence, Ginnie had earned Andrew's trust. She had treated him with respect, and without judgment, even as he had shared some of his most painful, shameful memories. For the first time in his life, he had been able to track the origins of his anger, exploring his early childhood experiences and the lineage of rage within his own family, all of which had given him useful information regarding his own temper and rage.

Stergios had likewise been an incredible resource. His expertise had assuredly shaped Andrew's understanding of the subject. He had provided thoughtful, unbiased data from his own research and knowledge of anger, violence, and rage, all of which had helped Andrew to deepen his own understanding. The final piece, Andrew realized, was an investigation into the broader cultural history of anger. Understanding the role anger played in society would allow him to contextualize both his own experiences and the observations he had gleaned from his medical colleagues. This project, however, represented a different, personal process. It would be solely Andrew's project.

Andrew leaned back in his chair, deep in thought. What was the origin and derivation of anger, he wondered. It was hard to imagine that man could predate anger. In all likelihood, anger predated man, although whether animals acted out of anger or survival instinct was a difficult question, perhaps even unanswerable.

Could the two be fully separated? In the quest for survival with limited resources, a certain amount of violence was necessary, but was that violence born of anger?

Where was the first written mention of anger, he wondered. Did it trace back to cave drawings? To Egyptian hieroglyphics? Again, he returned to the same question. How could one extract anger from necessary violence when the future of the human race was reliant upon hunting and killing, acts of violence not necessarily predicated on rage? Andrew turned on his computer and entered the University of New York's homepage.

Andrew, never a shrinking violet, decided to reach out to members of the liberal arts and classics faculty for guidance. The university was one of the country's leading academic institutions, a bastion of learning and a mecca for rational thought and free expression. It maintained a core curriculum for undergraduates that included courses in ancient history, archeology, psychology, and literature. The departments were extraordinary, the faculty respected for excellence around the world. Andrew surveyed department rosters, identifying individuals with knowledge about prehistoric times, the civilizations of ancient Egypt, Greece, and Rome, and the Renaissance period. He emailed several scholars, introducing himself as faculty at the medical school and explaining the details of his project as he requested their assistance.

When Andrew opened his email the following morning, he was pleased to see that two of his requests had been answered. The first response came from Professor Rostokovich, the second from Gustave Maranzini. A good start for certain!

Dr. Brown, I read your email with interest and would like to set up a time to speak. Would the day after tomorrow at 9 a.m. work for you? Best regards, Professor Wilhelm Rostokovich.

Andrew responded, and they coordinated a teleconference call for a couple days later.

Professor Maranzini similarly was intrigued, but he was in Europe doing research for a new book. He told Brown he would contact him upon his return in several weeks.

Wilhelm Rostokovich, a tenured professor at the University of New York, was a senior member of the Department of Archeology and an expert on prehistoric civilizations and culture. Andrew reviewed his bio and expertise and learned that Rostokovich had published extensively on early *Homo sapiens* and the Neanderthal man.

Andrew felt quite hopeful. If anger and violence were pervasive in prehistoric societies, he felt certain that Rostokovich would be able to provide valuable information, or at the very least be able to point him in the right direction.

Both Andrew and Rostokovich promptly began their teleconference exactly at 9.

"Good morning, professor! Thanks for taking the time to talk with me," Andrew began.

"Ah, good morning, Dr. Brown. Pleasure to meet you—albeit virtually. I must admit, I am intrigued by your project and interest in prehistoric man, but it seems so far removed from pediatric oncology. That is what you do, is it not?"

Rostokovich's virtual appearance was not what Andrew had anticipated. He was a young man in his mid-40s with close-cropped blond hair and nondescript features—certainly not the mad European scholar Andrew had expected.

Andrew explained his desire to trace the historical origins of anger through recorded history. He mentioned that he had previously investigated the psycho-emotional and physiological aspects of anger, the purported anger gene, and the pros and cons of rage and temper. He had not decided what to do with the products of his labor, he confessed, though perhaps he'd publish an article or a book. But that was a ways into the future. For now, he was merely chasing his own curiosity. Andrew omitted his personal connection and the overarching motivation beyond his work. Andrew could think of no good reason to discuss the circumstances regarding his administrative hold.

Rostokovich told Andrew that he would send him suggested reading material, but admitted he had not previously considered the issue of anger and its cultural presence or absence in Neanderthal man and *Homo sapiens*. "Give me a week or so, and I'll get back to you."

"Thanks, professor. May I call you by your first name?"

"Of course! Will is fine. You'll hear from me."

Several days later, Brown received an instant message from Will: *Andrew, I decided to investigate and see what I could uncover. The information is disjointed bits and pieces. I'll email you a summary of what I've learned. Are you free to speak now?*

Moments later, Andrew's mobile phone vibrated, classic jazz reverberating in his pocket.

Will provided Andrew with an ephemeral summary. The Neanderthals' civilization had originated 100,000 years ago in Africa before migrating to Asia and Europe about 60,000 years ago. The Neanderthal stereotypes in popular culture and the science community were consistent with nasty, violent lives, close-range hunting methods, and a violent, injury-prone social culture.

"Interpersonal relationships, however, actually demonstrated coexistence without anger and rage."

Rostokovich continued, telling Brown that remnants of Neanderthal DNA had been detected in the gene sequences of present day, 21st-century humankind. Fragments had been found in genetic materials that impact the immune system, metabolism, addiction, psychiatric disorders, mood, and behavior. Will surmised that Neanderthal genes were not necessarily agents of disease, but their existence in the brain correlated to detectable effects on behavior.

Before the day's end, Andrew received an email with an attachment from Rostokovich—17 pages of annotated notes, including comments and a list of references. Invaluable.

Andrew messaged Professor Rostokovich, thanking him profusely, and asked, "Will, might you by chance know about anger and rage in ancient Egypt?"

"Well, Andrew, today is your lucky day. Ancient Egyptian civilization and culture is one of my areas of expertise. I have an idea—why don't you come down to my office on the main campus? I'll order sandwiches and share my collection of Egyptian artifacts."

"Will," Andrew replied. "You're the best."

* * *

Andrew Brown always enjoyed a visit to the main campus of the University of New York; the noise, activity, and presence of students were exhilarating. The university was one of the oldest institutions of higher learning in the country, and Andrew always felt a sense of history and gravitas walking around its campus. Where else but the University of New York would he be able to find such willing and knowledgeable compatriots as Ginnie, Stergios, and now Will? All three at the top of their fields, all three willing to help Andrew in his intellectual exploration of anger.

Dodge Hall—home of the History, Anthropology, and Archeology departments—was located adjacent to the Cahill Library. It was a grand building, built in 1901 and framed by six massive Doric columns with 20 stone steps up from the quad to the entrance. No matter how many times he walked through, Andrew was awestruck by the building's majestic marble lobby with its domed stained-glass ceiling and white stone stairs. He paused for a moment to take in everything before walking up the stairs to Will Rostokovich's office.

The office door was ajar, and Will greeted Andrew warmly, as a friend and colleague. Will's office was like a museum. A prominent antique desk and three chairs dominated the space, surrounded by glass cases containing his collection of artifacts. Artwork adorned every available inch of the walls in his sanctum.

"Professor, your office is simply amazing."

"Let me show you around," Will said proudly.

He steered Andrew over to one of the glass cabinets that contained his prized Egyptian canopic jar collection. The jars had been used as part of the mummification process in which the stomach, intestines, lungs, and liver were removed from the dead body and preserved, as it was believed they would be needed in the afterlife. The jars were made of pottery and permanently sealed, with each depicting one of the four sons of Horus as guardians of the organ.

Andrew was surprised by how deeply moved he was by the jars. It was hard for him to wrap his brain around their antiquity. These jars had traveled continents and centuries, had borne witness to the dawn of industry and technology. Deep inside these jars, could there be the seeds of the origin of rage?

"Do the jars contain evil spirits?" he asked Will somewhat sheepishly. "If one is opened, will a malevolent spirit slip out?"

Will chuckled. "Well, some think so. Most scholars don't believe such tales, or at least wouldn't admit that they do. But stories have persisted for many centuries. To break the seal would be to disturb a peace set in place thousands of years ago."

Andrew nodded as he walked toward a glass display table containing amulets, rings, bracelets, and a necklace that was thought to possess magical protective powers for its holder. In the center of the case was a mummy mask carved of wood with delicate facial features and a gold-painted headdress.

Lastly, Andrew gazed at a large, framed document affixed to the wall behind the desk. He recognized that it was a reproduction of the Palette of Narmer, a 23-inch, small, green stone carved in the shape of a shield and etched with engravings and hieroglyphics. It was thought to be one of the first historical documents in the world, dating back to the 31st century BC.

"Professor Rostokovich, where and how did you accumulate such treasures?"

"Long and complicated story," Will replied with a laugh. "For another day. Let's talk about anger."

The professor told Andrew that an examination of ancient Egyptian literature identified overt sadness and happiness, whereas anger was controversial, less obvious, buried below the surface. Nevertheless, Will indicated that disagreement existed as archeologists discovered evidence of violence recorded on the walls of tombs attributed to Tutankhamen, Seti I, and

Ramses II. The drawings depicted the god Re who, frustrated with humans, decided to destroy them for their vices.

Will explained to Andrew that Re sent his eye in the form of the cow goddess Hathor, normally an animal linked to motherhood and nurturing, to destroy mankind. Re was therefore one of the gods associated with killing, as was the god Seth, considered to be the god of tempests. Isis, on the other hand, was not often linked to anger, though there were instances in which she expressed some anger. Horus was also associated with anger through his connection to the eye of Re sent to destroy humanity. The magical eye of Horus, which he lost during battle with his uncle Seth, became a very powerful amulet throughout most of ancient Egyptian civilization.

Will went on to say that in recovered Egyptian literature, rage was displayed by powerful humans such as kings, princes, and warriors aspiring to kingship. Anger was expected from powerful people. Rage, however, indicated a lack of control. For mortals at least, it was not proper to display or act upon rage, and as such, it was often punished by the gods or by fate.

Andrew had been so engrossed in their conversation that he had hardly noticed the sandwiches Will had ordered until the professor took a bite of his. Andrew likewise tried his BLT on rye—delicious!

Rostokovich continued. Anger, in Seth's case, was thought to have originated from a red cloud outside of his body. Egyptian writings used a number of images and metaphors to describe anger and rage, including the color red and the gepard, an ancient animal that resembled a cheetah.

For the better part of an hour, the two men continued their conversation, veering away from their focus on anger as Will shared other tangential pieces of his vast knowledge of ancient Egypt. It wasn't until Andrew's phone rang with a telemarketing call that either one noticed the time.

"Professor," Andrew said, rising from his seat, "you've helped immeasurably. I can't thank you enough, but I can't take up any more of your time."

"I could discuss this for hours," Will said with a laugh. "Please don't hesitate to reach out if you have any more questions as you continue your research."

"Certainly," Andrew said. "I would like it if we could stay in touch. By the way, do you know Gustave Maranzini? I was hoping to connect with him."

"I do," Will replied. "Can I assume then that ancient Greece is next on the list?"

Andrew nodded.

"Unfortunately, I believe Gustave is in Europe, researching his next book, and I don't believe he has teaching obligations for this coming semester. Don't wait for him. There should be tons of literature and scholarly articles on the topic. You should be able to find what you need on your own without difficulty."

"Yes, I suppose you're right," Andrew said. "I've just done some very preliminary research, and already I've found a quote from Aristotle that feels somewhat prophetic. 'Anybody can become angry, that is easy, but to be angry with the right person and to the right degree and at the right time and for the right purpose, and in the right way, that is not within everybody's power and is not easy.'"

"Prophetic indeed," Will agreed.

The two men shook hands and said their goodbyes. Andrew promised to pass along any findings of interest as he continued his research.

As he walked back to his office, Andrew continued to turn the Aristotle quote over and over in his mind. Homer and Plato had recognized that there were instances in which anger was not only tolerated but necessary—proper, even. They referred to anger as *thumos*, a part of Plato's model of the human soul. Achilles, the greatest of the Greeks, was the embodiment of *thumos*. One of the first known mentions of anger was in *The Iliad*, the foundation of Western literature and one of the first known pieces of writing. Not only did *The Iliad* deal thematically with anger, it seemed that the very first word of the epic was "anger." The entire plot was predicated on the *thumos* of Achilles, who had been wronged by King Agamemnon.

Achilles was the greatest warrior in the Achaean army, his status and worth inextricable from his ability to kill—his worth as a man was entirely dependent upon his brutality. But it was a brutality with context—violence within the rules and confines of war. During battle, the rage of Achilles and others might fly out of control. However, when the battle ended, the rage must again be harnessed.

Andrew considered this. It was a challenging if not unfamiliar paradigm. Within the context of certain situations mutually agreed upon within our societal contract, violent behaviors were not only acceptable but celebrated and encouraged, while those same behaviors elsewhere were deemed so unacceptable that they might land you on a leave of absence and a course for distressed physicians. Of course, Andrew hadn't brandished a sword in the middle of the University of New York, but wasn't it true that many of the traits that, when left to spiral out of control, turned into anger were the same traits that had helped him to find success as a doctor and in leadership? Certainly, he could be brash, direct, cut through the bullshit, and get to the root of the problem, but those were traits that, for the most part, had served him well. They'd given him the drive to pursue, to thrive, to ensure his own success and the success of his family.

Aristotle didn't consider anger to be uniformly or even generally bad. He maintained that there were times when a man ought to get angry, to feel the emotion and to act upon it. It was not simply a question of whether it was psychologically healthy for humans to express anger, nor was it an issue of prudently maintaining boundaries. According to Aristotle, anger was, at its very core, a moral issue, a matter of character.

Andrew understood that the purpose of his meetings with Dr. Parvich was not to eliminate these characteristics, but to temper them. Yet he wondered whether a rigid application of the principles of the ancient Greeks might diminish his ability to lead and perform his duties as a doctor to the best of his ability.

The Iliad seemed to recall a contest of ego between Achilles and King Agamemnon. Achilles asserted himself as the more powerful because of his prowess on the battlefield, whereas Agamemnon believed himself to be the more commanding because of his title and rule over the kingdom. Achilles, already believing Agamemnon to be an ineffective ruler, ultimately flew into a rage when he learned that the plague that had befallen the Achaeans was Agamemnon's fault. Ignoring the priest Apollo and forcibly taking Briseis (a "prize" woman whom Achilles had claimed as a fruit of war) angered the gods.

Within the context of the epic, violence and rage were depicted as a necessary fact of life through war, a natural response to the upending of what was right and fair. However, anger was transformed to a negative force when allowed to spiral out of control and evolve into rage—a liability.

This idea that anger or rage was a natural or even correct reaction to misrule and chaos was intriguing to Andrew. Wasn't it true that God, particularly in the Old Testament, was described as wrathful? He had grown up without practicing much religion but knew as well as anyone in the Western world that there were many sects of Christianity that worshipped an angry God of fire and brimstone.

Back in his office, another Google search led Andrew to a Christian blog, one entry in which sought to clarify the coexistence of both a loving and a wrathful God. The blog asserted that confusion lay in mistaking wrath for vengeance. God's wrath, the writer claimed, was a reaction to humanity's sins and the resultant upheaval of the natural order, much like Achilles's wrath. Like a loving parent, God's wrath was meant to teach, establish boundaries, and to demonstrate to his children—the entire human race—the difference between good and evil.

Of course, God's wrath ignited death, plagues, and the ultimate sacrifice of Jesus Christ. Again, Andrew internally rolled his eyes. All he'd manifested with his wrath was the word 'fuck.' Though he did think back to Camp Echo Sky, and the memory made him cringe. Fire and brimstone hadn't exactly been effective parenting tools that day with Serge. Perhaps his son had deserved some reprimand or punishment, but once Andrew had lost his temper, he'd also lost his credibility and his leverage.

Still, it was interesting that, woven so inextricably into the fabric of Western thought was an assumption, even an exaltation, of anger. Wasn't it the fear of God's rage that made so many Christians follow religious law and adhere to the moral standards set forth in the Bible? And wasn't that fear generally considered to be positive—something that led to a moral and just society?

So the threat of rage is somehow acceptable, while the actuality of it is not? Andrew thought.

Suddenly and inexplicably, an image came to Brown of a young Marlon Brando, his white shirt sleeves rolled up over his biceps, sweat on his forehead and danger in his eyes. The character of Stanley Kowalski in Tennessee Williams's iconic *A Streetcar Named Desire* was the picture of masculinity—tall, powerful, and *angry*. Kowalski's rage was his defining characteristic, the iron fist with which he ruled his small kingdom. Somehow, despite being verbally and physically abusive, an alcoholic, and a rapist, Kowalski remains an intriguing and attractive character, the quintessential Hollywood bad boy.

Even during the most memorable scene of the film, wherein Kowalski stands below his wife's window shouting, "Stella!" Kowalski is displaying aggression. He is shouting, barreling forward without asking permission, asserting his masculinity and ownership through violence.

In Kowalski's case, it seemed that his rage, like that of Achilles, stemmed from a perceived injustice. His wife's sister had come to stay and was taking up space in his home. She was eating his food, leaning on his hospitality, taking his wife's attention away from him, and disrespecting him. In Greek mythology, hospitality was necessary because one may never be sure whether their guest is a god, hidden in disguise. In the case of Stanley Kowalski, his limited hospitality had been overstretched, his guest had become unwelcome, and his rage served as a reaction to scarce resources. The presence of the sister-in-law upended the natural order of his world, and his reaction to that was rage.

It was easy to track the origin of Kowalski's rage, but Brown wondered whether there might be a broader understanding of the common origins of anger; whether there were emotions or specific types of situations that tended to trigger rage or anger.

He ran another Google search and discovered that anger was considered one of the six types of basic human emotions, along with happiness, sadness, fear, disgust, and surprise. According to this theory, all other emotions could be distilled down to the six basic emotions, and these six emotions could be combined and layered to build other emotions.

Under anger, the psychologists had written that, while it was generally considered to be a negative emotion, it could also have positive effects. For instance, anger can help clarify boundaries and serve as an important indicator that something is amiss in personal or professional relationships. An anger response essentially demonstrates to the person experiencing the emotion that something is not right, and their natural order has been upended.

That sounded familiar to Andrew.

Unsurprisingly, the site indicated that, while there are some positives to be gleaned, when allowed to spiral out of control, and especially when allowed to cross over into violence, anger is not a positive trait and could in fact be incredibly dangerous.

Further, the researchers wrote that prolonged anger could lead to disastrous health consequences, including high blood pressure, heart disease, chronic migraines, compounded stress, anxiety, and depression.

Andrew thought about his rage at Marissa over keeping cookies in the house. What good was a diet if he was going to give himself a heart attack anyway? He continued reading.

Though research found that the six basic emotions could not be further distilled, they could trigger one another. Shame, fear, frustration, and feelings of powerlessness often triggered anger. Andrew thought back to his own triggers. Perhaps part of his anger at Marissa when he cheated on his diet was actually shame and a feeling of powerlessness at his own inability to control his impulses. And frustration was certainly there also—at having the same fight about it each time.

When he thought back to that day in the driveway, he understood that frustration and powerlessness had been at the root of his anger. He was frustrated that no one was listening to him; he was frustrated at his powerlessness to control the situation. He didn't need a professional to tell him that he was someone who needed to be in control. In many ways, his entire profession was about maintaining control—over life, illness, and death. Losing that control, whether at home with his family or at the hospital with unnecessary red tape, led to intolerable feelings of helplessness. Instead, his brain adapted those feelings into one more palatable: anger.

There was something fundamentally wrong, even unfair, about this predicament. Wasn't the system designed to make people, men especially, seek control? American culture rewarded men who were able to provide for and take care of their families, both financially and physically. And in order to take care, didn't they need to maintain control? In that case, wasn't anger a natural reaction to loss of control?

Again, Andrew reminded himself that the goal was not to eradicate anger, but to mitigate it. And the more he thought about it, the better he felt. He could see that this issue was not unique to him. Yes, he had to take personal responsibility for his own inappropriate actions, but within the broader cultural context, he was beginning to understand where his feelings came from. It was not that he was abdicating responsibility—rather, he was learning *how* to take responsibility.

As he thought about this, he realized that he had been feeling a tremendous amount of shame around the rage itself—not just the rage but the leave of absence, his sessions with Dr. Parvich, the distressed physicians course. Reading and understanding the pervasiveness of anger throughout history helped him to release some of that shame, and he began to feel a weight lift.

This must be what addicts feel, he thought. *The shame around the behavior becomes its own weight, which becomes unbearable, setting the stage for that behavior to be repeated, and so on.*

A thought striking him, Andrew returned to his computer. It seemed of late—well perhaps not of late, but over the past few decades—that American political discourse had become increasingly angry, raging, and warlike. In the early 1990s, Rush Limbaugh and Newt Gingrich had established a scorched-earth style of political rhetoric, harnessing and weaponizing the anger of so many frustrated Americans who felt that they had been cheated by the system. Like Hitler in Nazi Germany, these extremists were happy to provide a scapegoat in the form of minorities, immigrants, or "feminazis." They tricked people into believing that there were limited resources, and that the reason they were unable to live the promise of the American Dream was because others were taking them away.

The reality, of course, was that those same politicians were deregulating and privatizing systems so that a handful of powerful men at the top of the totem pole hoarded the majority of the resources, leaving the rest to scramble for crumbs. It was a remarkable, if incredibly simple, sleight of hand. And in order to pull the wool over people's eyes, all these politicians and pundits needed to do was to tap into their anger, their rage at a system they felt had cheated them. That was how powerful the emotion was—the sense that something was fundamentally unfair changed the shape of a nation.

It seemed that this same frustration and feeling of impotence led to the dramatic uptick in acts of domestic terrorism. Columbine, the country's worst mass school shooting in a long time, had been executed by two bullied young men who felt powerless, helpless, and crushed by a system that was not working for them in the way that had been promised. In countless acts of domestic terrorism since, mostly young men had acted out their feelings of shame, frustration, and helplessness through violence, physically taking control over a situation or a perceived system over which they felt powerless.

Of course, the most clear and obvious manifestation of this was Donald Trump's rise to power, which awakened scores of angry white men across the country, resulting in acts of domestic terrorism in Charlottesville, Virginia and at the U.S. Capitol. Trump gave permission for frustrated men to point the finger of blame once again at minorities, immigrants, "feminazis," and Democrats—a bait and switch that ultimately enabled him to make off with millions.

The world today seemed to be increasingly apologetic and increasingly disingenuous. Hardly a day or week passed without a report of some public figure who had lost control, followed shortly by an insincere apology. It was popular to be anti-truth. The ambitious understood that anger was a tool to promote their own interests. However, like any tool, anger and rage had to be employed effectively—it was not a default solution. Effective anger was a precise and controlled strike. It was imperative that once unleashed, rage and violence be short-lived. Smoldering anger was not of value. Grudges were tiresome and time-consuming.

On a psychiatric website, Brown found an analysis that delineated between two fundamental personality types: those who become angry and those who are anti-anger. An "anti-anger" person does not fight. They are passive and more concerned with not upsetting others than with furthering their own interests. They possess debilitating empathy and sensitivity towards others. A "pro-anger" person always protects their interests. Though they are able to show empathy, sympathy, and mercy, they will always confront necessary conflict.

Brown checked his watch. The day was almost over. He felt both exhausted and exhilarated. It seemed to him that anger was foundational to American society, woven into the fabric of daily life, in politics, media, music, culture—even on the streets of New York City. Anger was ever-present, natural, useful even. However, his challenge would be knowing and understanding its limits—his limits. There was no denying the power of anger. As he'd acknowledged when he began his research, there was a place for anger—its origins underpinned other important drivers. But understanding and controlling it was crucial.

In a sense, it was much like practicing self-restraint in his diet. Anger and triggers were all around him and would continue to be all around him. There was no denying that. Try as he might, it would be impossible for him to control his surroundings to the extent that he could eliminate the causes and sources of anger. He felt confident, though, that as he continued his research and his work with Dr. Parvich, he could start to work toward establishing more control.

Brown stood, stretched, and looked down at the street below his window. It was rush hour now—the sidewalk even more bustling and the atmosphere even more charged as people pushed and shoved to make their way home. He packed up his briefcase, grabbed his keys, and headed out of the office to join the throng. Stepping out into the street, however, he felt a certain ease. The anxieties and pushiness of the people around him did not penetrate him as he made his way to his car in the garage.

When he arrived home, Marissa was in the kitchen cooking dinner. The last beautiful rays of sunshine cut through the kitchen window as aromas of fresh herbs and chicken wafted through the air. Marissa stood at the stove and Andrew stood behind her, wrapping his arms around her small frame.

"What's for dinner, honey?"

CHAPTER 19

RESIGNATION

The longer days, warmer temperatures, and flowering magnolias and dog-woods of spring were abruptly darkened by the arrival of the pandemic. The Coronavirus that had ostensibly begun in China ravaged the world, sparing no one. Every continent, country, and race was affected. In the United States, New York City immediately became the epicenter. The University of New York, along with every other city and state hospital, was overwhelmed. Hospital beds, intensive care beds, and emergency room capacities were inadequate. Oxygen tanks, respirators, masks, gowns, and face shields were all in short supply. The staff, nurses, and doctors were forced to multitask as the ever-increasing number of infected patients stressed the system beyond its limits. Walk-in patients lined up to be tri-aged, and the EMT service was swamped 24 hours a day, 7 days a week, bringing patients to the University of New York Medical Center coughing and unable to breathe. Many were placed on respirators before they even had vital signs taken.

Internists, emergency department doctors, and intensivists were crushed under the weight of the responsibilities that had been levied upon them. They worked with little rest and often for multiple days without time off. The cry for help was heard loud and clear. The solution: redeployment. Adaptability, resolve, and self-sacrifice were the only tools for fighting back.

Andrew Brown met the Centers for Disease Control and the New York State Department of Health criteria for increased risk of severe disease and death. He was a man over 65 years of age with preexisting medical conditions. The message was clear: Stay at home, isolate, work remotely. Fortunately, he was able to suspend patient care, and his colleagues and co-workers stepped in to support him. He and Marissa retreated to the safety of Rhinebeck as work became a series of Zoom meetings and conferences. Andrew's attire reverted to sweatpants, jeans, T-shirts, and sweaters in place of his usual suits, dress shirts, ties, and white coats.

Routine activities for the majority of doctors on the faculty came to a grinding halt. Elective surgery was canceled and non-urgent visits were postponed or converted to telemedicine. Only emergency care was rendered. The university hospital and medical center dramatically changed. The overcrowded parking garage sat empty, and the frenetic lobby was quiet. Research laboratories were shuttered, and ambulatory offices locked.

No playbook existed for this novel situation. Doctors and caregivers did what they could, but patients still died. The world remained laser-focused on COVID-19, while national leadership in Washington, D.C., remained inept—a repository of falsehoods and misinformation with science castigated and experts muffled.

The bucolic Hudson Valley outwardly appeared to be a safe haven far removed from the chaotic city, but every town and village was on lockdown. No shops or restaurants were open. Only the Hannaford food store and pharmacy permitted onsite shopping. However, the shelves emptied of essentials as soon as they were stocked. People were hoarding food, toilet paper, NSAIDs, and water—everything was scarce.

Despite being safely ensconced in his home office, Andrew was busy. He sat behind his large desk alongside its matching credenza—mid-century gems that Marissa had found at Brimfield, a famous summertime antique extravaganza in Massachusetts. His laptop, with its suddenly indispensable built-in camera and microphone, was connected to a 36-inch monitor that remained on day and night, helping Andrew to feel less far-removed. Practically the entire faculty of the Rose Children's Hospital, including members of the Division of Oncology, were working remotely and were in the hospital only when on service. Patient rounds, educational conferences, division and department meetings, leadership council, faculty updates, special events, alumni day, and celebrations all took place via Zoom. If orchestrated properly, the virtual computer conferences possessed a certain intimacy and attendance far exceeded the in-person proceedings—one ray of light in a dark void.

Eventually, the onerous lockdown protocols and masking guidelines enforced by New York City and New York State began to produce positive results. The number of COVID cases, hospitalizations, and deaths began to wane.

By late summer, the University of New York began to allow less restrictive operations, and Andrew and his colleagues began to return to the hospital, where, suddenly, everything was different. Gaining entrance to the building required a negative rapid-PCR test, and the pandemic remained at the forefront of everyone's minds. Although patients resumed cancer therapy, everyone was isolated from one another in cubicles or behind curtains. No visitors were allowed—only essential workers and a single parent or guardian with each patient, meaning no child-life specialists, no psychosocial and integrative therapy services, and no administrative personnel.

The once bustling, upbeat atmosphere of the child and adolescent oncology outpatient floor was suddenly nonexistent. To speak with a patient, take a history, or do a physical exam, Andrew and his colleagues donned gowns, masks, and face shields with their masked patients. Andrew felt physically present, but not engaged. Patient care was not the same. He had always enjoyed caring for patients, but this was different. The experience lacked intimacy. The pandemic had changed everything.

On a Thursday morning in September, Andrew was in the Oncology Clinic early, a little before 7:30. The monthly Zoom faculty meeting led by Jeff Flack wasn't set to begin until 8, but Andrew needed to have some blood work drawn before his visit with his internist the following Tuesday. The oncology nurses, several of whom Andrew had worked with for more than 25 years, were superb, skillful blood drawers, and whenever he needed blood work, he asked Corrine, Beth, Angela, or Mayra to take the sample.

They were all happy to oblige. However, EPIC, the new electronic medical record at the University of New York, had added a complicating wrinkle beyond registration, reproducing labels, and drawing blood. Now, orders needed to be verified via scanned barcodes, identification wrist bands, and preprinted documentation. In short, an ordeal manifested.

When Dr. Brown arrived, he found Angela seated alone at the nurses' station on her computer, logged into EPIC. "Angela, would you do me a quick favor and check to see if orders for blood work are in my chart?"

Angela indicated that she did not believe she could enter Brown's chart because he was an employee and access would be denied.

"Understood." Brown said, "Just try."

After clacking away on her keyboard, she replied, "No luck. The system won't let me in. Sorry, Dr. Brown."

Frustrated, Andrew walked quickly into clinic workroom, well aware that that the 8 o'clock hour was fast approaching. He asked Kim, a nurse practitioner for the brain tumor team, if she would assist him and show him how to log in, check orders, print labels, etc. She did, but the connection between the Kim's computer and the printer malfunctioned. Andrew and Kim attempted to print to a second printer in the workroom, but with no luck. Finally, they located a third printer at the nurses' station that received the wireless instructions. Success, but precious time had been lost. The faculty meeting had already started, and Andrew still had no needle in his vein.

Andrew retrieved the printed stickers, affixed them to the Vacutainer tubes, and asked Joanna, the phlebotomist, if she would draw the blood.

"Of course! Come into my room and take a seat."

Joanna wiped Andrew's arm with an alcohol swab, placed the orange rubber tourniquet around his biceps, and deftly drew the blood, filling six tubes.

As he flexed his bandaged arm, Andrew thanked Joanna and retreated to his office to listen to the remaining 30 minutes of the faculty meeting.

Thursday afternoons from noon to 3 o'clock were reserved for divisional conferences, the weekly tumor board, the morbidity and mortality conference, and the oncology patient conference. As per pandemic protocol, all meetings remained virtual. Zoom conferences required participants to sign into the meeting and to disconnect at its conclusion. Occasionally, a participant would forget to disconnect and sign off or to mute themselves, making what might otherwise be a private phone call public to anyone remaining on the line. The potential for an embarrassing slip-up was high.

That afternoon, the divisional conference was ending, with people signing off and disconnecting from Zoom. Before he had disconnected, however, Fred Morris, the division director, answered a phone call from Patty Parisa, the head of nursing for Pediatric Oncology.

Andrew was just about to sign off when he heard his name. Fred had Patty on speakerphone.

"I have to tell you that Andrew Brown lost his temper this morning." Patty was strong and direct. "Corrine is lodging a complaint. I have already reported this to Andrea Rognolia."

Immediately, Andrew messaged Morris.

This is bullshit, he wrote. *I have no idea what is going on, but there was no temper, no anger. This is ridiculous. You must immediately put a stop to this insanity.*

Morris disconnected the Zoom conference and told Brown he would try to help him. But Brown knew it was too late. A formal complaint had already been lodged. The damage was done.

Morris called Andrew and told him that that the nurses had reported being pressured by him to enter his EPIC personal record. "They have no access to your chart, and had you persisted, they could have been exposed to disciplinary action, including suspension."

Brown told Morris that he had pressured no one, of that he was certain. When Angela indicated that she could not comply, Kim had assisted him in properly finding the orders, using the barcodes, and printing the identification wristband and labels. He had been frustrated, as he wanted to be on time for the faculty meeting and the printers were offline, but he assured Morris that he had done nothing inappropriate. He was sure there had not been one iota of bad behavior or anger.

"You're the chief, Fred…Can't you put a stop to this?"

"It's too late," Morris said.

After a hasty goodbye, Andrew hung up.

Not again.

He couldn't believe this was happening. He received an email from Barry Steinglass inviting him to a Zoom conference the next day at 10. "Invitation" seemed to be the wrong word. Andrew responded affirmatively. He knew the topic of discussion. He messaged Jeff Flack, the department chair, but he was not available until Friday afternoon and promised to call Brown at 3 o'clock.

Andrew Brown signed into the Zoom call early. Other than Steinglass, he did not know the identity of the other participants on the call. Promptly at 10 o'clock, the circular connecting symbol appeared, and Steinglass introduced Louise Lange, vice president of nursing at Rose Children's Hospital, and Gladys Gallagher from hospital human resources.

In unison, they said, "Good morning, Dr. Brown."

"Good morning."

Louise Lange ran the virtual conference call and told Brown that several nurses on the Pediatric Oncology floor had lodged complaints against him for inappropriate behavior that had to be investigated completely.

Brown was incredulous. He maintained his innocence, telling the other participants that he had done nothing inappropriate. Perhaps he had been a bit short with the nurses in his desire to get back in time for his meeting, but beyond that, any further allegations were an exaggeration if not an outright lie. As he talked, he grew increasingly agitated, frustrated by the unfairness of the situation. He told them that he had no idea what was motivating Corrine.

"Frankly, truth be told, she is flat-out not a good person and creates an atmosphere of hostility, control, and rancor," Andrew said, properly angry now. "I want to lodge a formal complaint against Corrine. I will enumerate the charges, put them in writing, and email them to you all as soon as this call is complete. I assure you that I did nothing wrong. This is crazy."

Gladys Gallagher told Brown that he could not lodge a countercomplaint. The University of New York Hospital bylaws prohibit an accused person from levying a neutralizing response.

Brown said, "Let me get this straight. Someone can accuse me of wrongdoing, but if I tell you the allegation is unfounded nonsense and want to raise my concerns regarding the creation of a hostile environment, I am unable to do so?"

"That's correct. You are not permitted retribution."

"Where is the fairness in that?"

"That's just the way it is," Gallagher said.

* * *

When Flack called Friday afternoon, Andrew was still upset but calmer, recognizing that now was not the moment for anger. Flack was up to speed, having had discussions with Steinglass and Fred Morris. Andrew told his boss, colleague, and friend that he was shocked. He recounted the entire incident to Jeff in detail. He already had pages of notes and remembered every word, comment, facial expression, and intonation. He told Flack that he had been hypervigilant about his behavior secondary to past incidents and assured Jeff that under no circumstances would he lose his temper or display anger. Andrew admitted that he had asked Angela to enter his EPIC chart to verify orders for blood tests, but upon learning she was not able to confirm, he had thanked her and gone to another computer station where, with Kim's assistance, he did it himself.

Flack recommended that he do nothing for the moment. He would speak with Steinglass again and reach out to Dean Smith for her council. He urged Andrew to be cool—no discussion, no confrontation. They would speak again on Monday afternoon.

"Remember," he advised, "for now, do nothing."

Saturday afternoon, Brown composed and sent an email to Flack, Steinglass, Olivia Smith, and Louise Lange. He apologized for his indiscretion regarding his request to ask a nurse to enter his EPIC chart against her protestations. He acknowledged that he had been wrong, but assured them all again that he had not, under any circumstances, lost his temper, become angered, or used profanity.

Andrew hoped that his contrition and admission of wrongdoing would end the incident once and for all. He soon realized that would not be the case. Not even close.

Sunday evening, Brown received an email from Steinglass requesting they speak first thing Monday morning.

The following morning, the caller ID announced Steinglass's call at 9 o'clock. "Andrew—good morning."

"Good morning, Barry."

For a brief moment, Andrew thought he was about say that all was fine, sorry for the misunderstanding. Instead, Steinglass said, "I have to put you on administrative leave and hold your privileges. No patients...you know the drill."

It took every ounce of restraint Brown possessed not to express his true feelings. He whispered in a barely audible voice, "This is outrageous. I did nothing wrong."

Steinglass told Brown that was not what he had heard, and the situation needed a complete and thorough investigation. He asked Brown if he routinely had personal blood work drawn by the outpatient nurses.

Andrew confirmed, saying that for more than 25 years the nurses in the Oncology Clinic had been willing to draw blood work when needed, once or twice a year. Not once did anyone ever complain. Not once did any of the nurses indicate that they felt uncomfortable or refuse to assist.

"Look, Barry, this is outrageous. What you are suggesting is unfathomable. I am telling you that nothing untoward transpired, yet you are choosing to believe the nurse and totally disregard my word."

"Andrew, I'm sorry. I have no other option. Nursing is forcing the issue. Even if I wanted to take your word, I can't. Procedures must be followed. You're out, on hold, no patients."

Andrew took a deep breath. He tried to sit on his proverbial wall, but suddenly he simply could not hold back anymore. "This incident is fiction! Contrived!" he said, his voice filled with released emotion. "The nurse involved is a bad egg. She belittles people routinely, especially the fellows and nurse practitioners, yet I am on administrative hold, and the alleged accuser will not experience any repercussions. Let me ask you, Barry, do you think she understands the results and complexities of her complaint? Do you think she understands the abject power she possesses, the control that she wields? Do you think she understands that at this moment in time my career resides in her hands?"

Brown took a breath and then continued.

"Did the chairman of the Department of Neurology who walked out of a faculty practice meeting with a boisterous 'Fuck this, I'm out of here,' suffer any repercussions? No, he didn't. Did the surgeon who threw a clamp across the operating room and berated the circulating nurse and yelled, 'Fuck this!' suffer repercussions? No, he didn't. Did the violent tirade made by the director of the clinical laboratories, replete with four-letter expletives, result in any remonstrations? No, *it didn't*."

He paused again.

"I ask you, Barry, why I am being singled out? Why am I on administrative hold? Why am I being investigated? I'll tell you why. Because someone complained—that is the common denominator. Think about the process, Barry. There is a disconnect. There's no consistency. A seemingly egregious incident for one individual is passed over by another, and no complaint registered. And forgive me, but what is even more unbalanced is the inability of the alleged accused to have his voice heard in an equal opportunity to respond. I am not referring to retribution, but an equal opportunity to be heard. Look, I do not want to seem melodramatic, but this is serious stuff. This is this how my professional life ends. I'm not going through the embarrassment or humiliation again. I have nothing else to say. Goodbye, Barry."

Hanging up the phone, Andrew was beyond angry. He felt persecuted. He was seething—temples bulging, heart racing.

What the fuck is going on here?

* * *

"Fuck" was the word that had begun Dr. Brown's voyage into the abyss.

But although historically the word may be considered obscene, even offensive and vulgar by some, it is ever so slowly gaining acceptance. "Fuck" has become more publicly tolerable, an example of the dysphemism treadmill wherein former vulgarities become inoffensive and commonplace. The origins of the word are obscure. Although the word in its literal sense refers to sexual intercourse, its most common usage is figurative, frequently used to amplify and convey disdain, to indicate the speaker's strong sentiment, and to offend or shock the listener. In terms of its parts of speech, "fuck" has a very flexible role in English grammar, functioning as both a transitive and intransitive verb, and as an adjective, adverb, noun, and, of course, an interjection.

In the *Oxford English Dictionary*, more than 100 different senses, usages, and collocations—fuck around, fuck you, fuck me, fuck it—are identified for 'fuck', as well as its derived forms—fucker, fuckee, fuckability—and compounds—fuckfest, fuckhole, fuckface.

The modern usage of "fuck" was established by the mid- to late 19th century and has been fairly consistent ever since. But according to some linguistic experts, enduring cultural models informing our beliefs about the nature of sexuality and sexual acts preserve its status as a vile utterance that continues to inspire moral outrage.

In 1928, English writer D.H. Lawrence's novel *Lady Chatterley's Lover* gained notoriety for its frequent use of the words "fuck" and "fucking." First published in the United States in 1951, *The Catcher in the Rye* by J.D. Salinger featured the first use of "fuck you" in print. The novel remains controversial to this day due in part to this. The word began to break into cinema when it was uttered once in the film *Vapor* in 1963, and in two Andy Warhol films, *Poor Little Rich Girl* and *My Hustler* (both 1965). In 1967, the British film *Ulysses* utilized the word several times, and American director Robert Altman used the word "fuck" for the first time in a major American studio film in *M*A*S*H* (1970).

The word is now a permanent fixture in modern vernacular. It is spoken by children, adolescents, and adults alike. It is spoken in school, in the workplace, and in the home. Many use the word routinely and often without malice. Some continue to be offended while others are not.

When Andrew Brown said, "Fuck this shit," it was not directed at anyone, but it was rather a sign of situational frustration. Yet the repercussions of the word's utterance were severe and immediate. How many times a day at the University of New York, with a workforce of 10,000 faculty and staff healthcare providers, is "fuck" spoken? Perhaps hundreds, if not thousands of times. It is spoken by physicians, department chairs, surgeons, administrative leadership, therapists, nurses, men, and women. Where is the equipoise, the fairness? The university handbook may state that vulgar language is prohibited, but is that policy really enforced in a regular, consistent fashion? A single incident may be reported and sent up the chain, resulting in far-reaching consequences, while other instances are passed by unnoticed.

The issue remains that the obscenity is offensive to some and not to others. There is no universal standard policy, and there *should* be. There must be. To mandate that "fuck" and other "obscenities" never be uttered is not only unenforceable, it's infeasible.

* * *

Andrew heaved a heavy sigh. His entire predicament was incomprehensible. At the time of the previous incident, he could at least pinpoint his indiscretion, and had agreed that his behavior had been inappropriate. But he had paid his dues and put in the work to change. His time with Ginnie and at the distressed physicians course had been challenging, but the experiences had pushed him to grow. Had it all been for nothing?

A text from Jeff Flack flashed across Andrew's cell, asking him to call his office. When Jeff picked up, the exhaustion in Andrew's voice was obvious.

"Jeff," he said, "I can't. I can't go through another administrative timeout, let alone a potential medical board inquiry with a lawyer. I don't want a blemish on my record." He took a deep breath. "Jeff, what would happen if I resigned from the hospital? Is that possible?"

The pandemic had altered patient care. It was no longer fun or enjoyable, and the relationships between doctors and their patients were dramatically different.

The two discussed the matter from every possible vantage point. Andrew, like most pediatrics faculty at Rose Children's Hospital, was employed by the University of New York rather than by the hospital.

Andrew told Jeff that the only thing he would be giving up was one outpatient session per week. He reminded Flack that he no longer participated as an inpatient attending on the Oncology Service. All of his responsibilities, everything he did as vice chair of Outreach and Development—the creation of the specialist webinars, flyers, brochures, email newsletters, annual reports, and philanthropy—could be done virtually.

"Frankly, Jeff, what would I lose? What would we lose?" Brown answered his own question: "Nothing."

"It's certainly an interesting idea." Jeff asked Andrew to give him a day or so to flesh it out and determine if it was even possible. He thought it seemed reasonable, but he needed to be certain there would be no unforeseen ripple effects. "I'll speak to Dean Smith and Steinglass," Jeff said. "Let's touch base tomorrow."

That evening, Marissa and Andrew enjoyed a calm, restful evening together in their Rhinebeck home. She prepared a dinner of chicken Marsala with a green salad. As they ate, Andrew told his wife and partner of almost 45 years what he had discussed with Jeff Flack.

"Marissa," he said. "I think this change will be great for me. I hope Flack agrees. I'm exhausted, yet excited."

Marissa agreed. "Ever since you started your work with Ginnie, you've seemed much happier, calmer." She took his hand over the table. "I think it's time for you to move on and start this next chapter. Why stay in a stressful environment that could potentially ignite anger? What's the point?"

Flack called first thing the next morning. "Andrew, I think this is going to work. Olivia Smith is on board, and frankly this maneuver makes things easy for Steinglass…Not that we care, but he agreed as well."

Flack instructed Andrew to send a one-sentence email to Steinglass resigning from the University of New York Hospital effective immediately, dated that day.

Written, sent, done.

Jeff told Andrew that he would receive an email from him with a letter attached memorializing their discussion and guaranteeing full compensation and benefits. The letter was received before the end of the day.

Andrew and Flack discussed a two-year phased retirement, a university-permitted contractual agreement among the dean, department chair, and senior faculty in good standing to plan for the next chapter in their careers. Andrew told Jeff that he would like to initiate an arrangement that would allow him to retire on his terms in June 2022 at the age of 76.

Although Andrew Brown maintained his innocence and continued to question the process, he also felt relieved.

Retirement would be a wholly new challenge, but one he looked forward to. It would mean more time with Marissa and the grandchildren, more time on the golf course, and more time to spend on charitable work. He could leave the ugly drama and bureaucracy of the hospital behind and enjoy the life he had built for himself and his family. He would be able to continue to work remotely, fulfill his responsibilities as Vice Chair for Outreach and Development, and continue his philanthropic work with his charity. Most importantly, he had crafted a path forward for the end of his long, productive career.

Andrew Brown's experiences with anger and his journey to learn of its complexities were profound. He was a different man, older and perhaps wiser. Andrew recalled a quote from Mahatma Gandhi that summarized and condensed his understanding of anger and rage. It provides an example of how anger may be exploited and conquered.

Sitting in the sunroom with Marissa one fine evening, Andrew said, "I have learned through bitter experience the one supreme lesson to conserve my anger. As heat conserved is transmuted into energy, even so our anger controlled can be transmuted into a power that can move the world."

EPILOGUE
RETIREMENT

Retirement was an adjustment for Andrew Brown, which required a reordering of priorities. He found it difficult, not unlike a race car decelerating from 150 miles per hour to 10. He had enjoyed a full, productive career for many years, and now it was about to come to what he considered to be a successful end. He had treated thousands of children and adolescents; earned a reputation nationally for his leadership in designing and running clinical trials in patients with leukemia and lymphoma; built a novel Division of Oncology at the University of New York; and mentored the careers of countless young colleagues, who'd go on to further his many causes. Yet, as he stood in his office gathering mementos, books, awards, photographs, and degrees, it felt bittersweet.

Andrew was aware of the clichés describing how one should retire from work but not from living a full life, and so on. Though the adages were plentiful, most were too trite to be of much help or comfort.

Andrew found himself unable to simply ease into retirement. It was not his modus operandi. His doctorly inclinations still intact, he believed preparation mandatory. Though he was disciplined and calculating, there were numerous unanswerable questions and variables that would impact his retirement, most of which he was unable to control.

Health and well-being were at the top of the list, followed closely by other considerations—finances, downsizing, lifestyle, travel, and maintaining friendships and relevance. Several of the issues would take care of themselves, evolving over time with no intervention or premeditated thought required. Others were dictated by circumstances—personal or otherwise—and existed beyond Andrew's control. Andrew believed that the foundation for the present was rooted in the past, whereas the present provides the path forward for the future.

A successful and meaningful retirement would require effort. It necessitated significantly more than gardening, playing golf, exercising, reading *The New York Times*, and spending time with his grandchildren. All pleasant and enjoyable activities, for certain, but not the path forward for long-term happiness. On this front, Brown determined two potential avenues to consider. The first was personal gratification—things of importance for himself, Marissa, and the family. Second was service to community—he wanted to remain useful and relevant.

Andrew and Marissa enjoyed their Dobbs Ferry apartment. It was close to the University of New York and to the grandchildren, and it was an easy ride from there to Rhinebeck, but Andrew wondered if it was necessary. After a long discussion with Marissa, they agreed that they should give up the apartment and relocate permanently to the Hudson Valley. They were in no rush and decided to wait to move until the landlord was able to rent out the apartment.

As it happened, this did not take long. Margaret showed their two-bedroom apartment the next weekend, and the first couple who viewed it signed a new lease that very day. The only issue, the landlord explained, was that the new tenants wanted to take occupancy the first week of June…in less than a month.

"Not possible," Marissa said simply. "We don't even have a moving company. It can't be done."

Andrew considered, then said, "I think we can do it, honey. I'll call Mike at Blue Eagle Movers. They can do everything. Moving is hard enough, and we're not as young as we used to be. We'll do just the important valuables and let them take care of everything else. Don't stress."

Marissa agreed, albeit somewhat reluctantly, and Andrew called Mike first thing the next morning. He explained the situation and asked if Blue Eagle could do the job.

"For you, doc? Of course."

That evening, Andrew and Marissa had dinner at a local Italian bistro. The Browns had a connection to Carmella's. Fifteen years earlier, the pediatric oncology team at the hospital had treated nine-year-old Lucia Carmella, the daughter of the restaurant owner, Luigi. Lucia tragically succumbed to a metastatic pelvic Ewing's sarcoma, and less than six months after being diagnosed. Though Luigi and his wife Maria remained grief-stricken to this day, they were eternally grateful to Andrew and considered him a friend, doting on him whenever he and Marissa visited the restaurant.

Cutting into her grilled branzino, Marissa said, "Honey, I realized today that as we consolidate two homes into one, we have two of pretty much everything! Not only furniture, but TVs, linens, and an entire kitchen and dishes, not to mention clothes."

"I know. I've been thinking about that too."

"We can ask Pia and Serge to take anything they want," Marissa said.

"Well, sure," Andrew said, "But what about the rest?"

Andrew dismissed the idea of storage. It would be expensive, and what would they be saving the items for anyway?

Neither Andrew or Marissa had the will or know-how to attempt navigating online marketplaces, and an estate sale would have people traipsing in and out of the house—out of the question, certainly.

They settled on donations to local charities. In the end, it was the logical choice.

The Friday before Memorial Day, Mike and his 12-man crew arrived just before 8 in the morning. Andrew and Marissa had managed to pack their personal effects and valuables beforehand. Marissa had wrapped and boxed the Lalique glass art collection, the Daum crystal figurines and decorative glassware, and her assortment of antique Roseville vases and jewelry. The smaller guys did the packing, while the larger among them loaded the truck. Amazingly, the entire contents of the apartment—clothes, two sets of dishes, the wedding crystal and silverware, every kitchen accoutrement, wine collection, pantry contents, furniture, paintings, mirrors, and lamps—were completely packed and loaded onto the trucks before noon.

And with that, they were ready for their move to Rhinebeck.

The trucks arrived at Ravine Road shortly before 2 o'clock. Andrew greeted the Blue Eagle crew with lunch from the local pizza shop, a gesture the men appreciated as their day was only half over.

Working at warp speed, the guys cleared half the garage, relocated the farm table, banquette, love seats, chairs, a sofa, two beds, mattresses, mirrors, cabinets, rugs, and so much more. They positioned the items from the apartment in the appropriate rooms and stacked 93 boxes—a lifetime of possessions—in the downstairs guest bedroom. Unpacking and sorting through the boxes would be a monumental task for another day. There was no rush. They had the rest of their lives, after all.

Mike and the Blue Eagle men finished at 5 p.m. He reviewed the packing list and invoice with Andrew, saying as he finished, "Everything look good, doc?"

Andrew wrote a personal check for just over $6,000 and handed it to Mike. "Your guys were amazing. Thanks."

With the movers gone, the house suddenly felt strangely quiet.

"Marissa, let's do dinner at Basil and Thyme."

"Good," Marissa sighed. "I'm exhausted. I couldn't bear cooking right now."

Basil and Thyme, a local Indian restaurant, was a favorite of the Browns. Andrew ordered appetizers, *lasuni gobi*, dried cauliflower, and vegetable *samosa*. Marissa favored the Goan fish curry, while Andrew adored the *navratan korma*—vegetables in a creamy cashew and almond sauce and a healthy side of garlic *dal*.

Pausing in mid-feast, Marissa looked up at Andrew. "Honey, I know moving and retiring is stressful, but I need you to promise me something. Please don't stress out. We'll get everything done. We've got nothing but time to unpack and sort through a lifetime of treasures. Just promise you won't freak out on me. Please be patient."

Recalling the lessons he had learned from Nashville and his sessions with Ginnie Parvich, Andrew smiled. "I'll try to be calm and curb my frustration. No anger, no temper. If I feel it coming, I know what to do. I'll sit on the wall, take deep breaths, and walk away."

It was a perfect evening.

The next morning, Andrew was up at sunrise. He went to the garage and photographed, listed, and estimated the value of its contents, necessary to procure a professional appraisal. He forwarded the information to On-Line Value Appraisal, to whom he paid a small fee on Venmo and within the hour received a documented, certified valuation.

Gary Reilly arrived with his son, Gary Jr., at 9 o'clock. Father and son helped Marissa relocate the baby grand piano, replace three carpets with Oriental area rugs, and reposition the decorative *étagère* shelving in the living room that would ultimately house the Lalique, Daum, and other collectibles.

When they'd finished, they loaded their 12-foot van with the garage's contents and covered, strapped, and secured the Browns' belongings in place. Andrew followed Gary's van to the Goodwill store on Route 9G, a 15-minute drive. Margaret Quinn, the store manager, expected them, having been forewarned by Andrew. Margaret guided the movers to empty the truck and put everything in the rear of the store. She did a quick assessment to reconcile the items with Brown's list.

"Everything seems in order, Dr. Brown." Ms. Quinn stamped and signed the tax receipt, saying, "Thank you so much for your incredible kindness. Your donation will help so many families throughout the Hudson Valley. We're so grateful to you and Mrs. Brown."

Andrew mentioned that as he and Marissa emptied and sorted through the boxes, they would make additional donations of clothes, kitchen appliances, dishes, and rugs. "We have so much and are pleased to know that we will be helping others less fortunate."

The process was slow, but bit by bit the country house came together. Andrew remained under control, and even relatively relaxed. Lessons had been learned, and perhaps, he thought, he really had changed for the better.

The next hurdle was the family finances. Although Marissa had an IRA and a few well-performing stocks, their greatest source of income was Andrew's 401k from the University of New York. Fortunately, the balance represented sufficient funds for the future. The entire allocation was in a Vanguard target retirement fund of mixed stocks and fixed income. It was relatively safe, and while the gains were modest, the losses in a downturn were also less severe. Andrew told Marissa he was ill-prepared and uncomfortable with managing their retirement income, investments, expenses, and debt.

"I think we should speak to a financial planning manager. There is a lot at stake, and I just can't live with financial uncertainty."

Andrew contacted Rich Carlisle, a good friend and the president of Alpine Palisade Capital Management, for advice. Carlisle introduced him to Gil Vincent, the director of the personal wealth management section of the firm, whom he met over Zoom.

"Dr. Brown, it's a pleasure to meet you, if virtually. Rich filled me in. My team and I are looking forward to working with you. We'll help guide your financial future. I'm going to email you a questionnaire, contract, fee schedule, and information about our services. Review everything, and we'll schedule a time to jump on a Zoom call and get started."

The documents from Alpine Palisade were extensive. They requested more personal information about the Browns than any person or entity had previously—well beyond assets and expenses. According to Gil, an accurate prediction of the future necessitated as much family information and history as the Browns were able to provide. Gil asked for a laundry list of backup records, past and present tax returns, pay stubs, bank statements, brokerage accounts, and a complete and accurate accounting of debt, including statements from each creditor. Importantly, Vincent asked about retirement income, Social Security, and any additional sources of revenue.

There were queries about lifestyle preferences, travel, estimates regarding formidable expenditures, and the importance of gifting to children and grandchildren. Alpine Palisade took this exercise seriously.

At first glance, the approach seemed formulaic—plug in the numbers, adjust for actuarial predictions of survival at three- to five-year increments, and create models for the future. The Browns would soon understand that the complexity was significantly more profound.

Where to begin? Andrew calculated every expense, from the mortgage to insurance, automobile leases, utilities, heating oil, landscaping, snow removal, pool service, and so on. Revenue would be less predictable and less assured. Andrew had two retainer contracts, the first as a medical expert assisting Borden Lawrence Price, a Denver law firm, to vet potential cases; the second as a consultant helping the Davis Caldwell Foundation to identify children's charities worthy of donations.

Most importantly, Andrew anticipated a part-time position with Heroes for Hope, a charitable organization he had founded 25 years prior with his friend and colleague Rich Carlisle. The organization raised much-needed funds to support the pediatric cancer program at the University of New York, and since its inception, had raised $100 million for patient and family services, clinical program development, research, education, endowed professorships, and recruitment and retention of faculty. The foundation was one of Andrew's most relevant and long-lasting accomplishments. He was enormously proud of its contributions, which had helped countless doctors, healthcare providers, and families afflicted by child and adolescent cancer.

The Alpine Palisade team scrutinized, modeled, and remodeled the information and data. They created several different algorithms that ranged from aggressive investing and asset depletion to a more conservative approach with the goal of maintaining lifestyle and providing sufficient resources for the future, children, and grandchildren. Gil Vincent forwarded the Alpine Palisade documents to Andrew and Marissa for their review and scheduled a Zoom call to discuss their suggested financial plans and to answer questions.

The virtual conference call went exceedingly well. The theme was consistent with Andrew's paradigm: Conserve and preserve. Gil was focused and firm in his recommendations. He suggested a budget that encompassed an extremely conservative approach that relied heavily on income from Andrew's retainer agreements, Heroes for Hope, and Social Security. He strongly urged Brown to continue long-term health insurance that would provide for a nursing home or in-home care services when needed but to discontinue term life insurance, as the cost was prohibitive. Vincent advocated maintaining the Vanguard 401k in a neutral position, if possible, at least for the time being. The gains would be modest—5 to 6 percent, with a comparable draw-down of approximately equal value.

Marissa asked about major expenditures such as travel, home improvements, and disbursements to the children and grandchildren.

"Yes, of course," Gil said. "The goal is to allow you to maintain a lifestyle that is comfortable and secure, but you have certainly earned the right to enjoy retirement. My personal philosophy is that these years should encompass the space between 'no longer' and 'not yet.'"

Andrew wanted to gift Pia and Serge the Internal Revenue Service maximum allowable annual allocation. "I want the children to have the funds now, when they can put them to good use. I'd like them to have money to buy a house, make renovations, travel, go to whatever school they'd like. I want to do it now rather than wait until Marissa and I are deceased."

"We can make that happen," Gil said, nodding.

Vincent stressed an important concept of retirement planning. "What seems appropriate and sound today may require sudden alterations. Even the best-laid plans of mice and men can go awry. Expenses and income sources are likely to evolve over time, but the most significant variable will be your health and well-being. A major life-threatening health crisis or sudden death will necessitate an immediate reassessment. There is no way to plan for such an event, other than to be aware that the possibility is always there. Therefore, we will make adjustments every three to five years as needed," Vincent explained.

"Understood."

"Okay, any final comments, thoughts, questions?"

"No, I think we're good."

Gil told the Browns that he would have his team at Alpine Palisade prepare paperwork with detailed plans. "Give us a few weeks, and we'll reconvene. Good meeting this morning. I look forward to working with you both!"

With retirement finances under control, the next challenge for Andrew to tackle was time. Retirement afforded Andrew and Marissa an opportunity to be together and share experiences like day trips to museums, concerts, and Broadway shows. In retirement, the Browns could be tourists.

Spending as much time with Will and Clara as possible was right at the top of Andrew's list. It was a short drive from Rhinebeck to their daughter's home in Pleasantville, less than 90 minutes. There would also be time for gardening, planting, transplanting, and pruning. Regular exercise was, of course, a must. Peloton classes four to five days a week were already a part of Andrew's routine, and good for the mind, body, and waistline. He particularly enjoyed the 30- to 45-minute rides along the Pacific Coast Highway, and the fauna of Hawaii.

Golf would be a regular activity, as well. He would practice his short game, pitching, and chipping. Reading was mostly nonfiction or historical fiction, with an occasional John Grisham and Ken Follett novel added for good measure. And friends and an active social life were, of course, important.

Andrew recognized the curse of idle time. He was committed to making retirement the next phase of the journey, not the end, not the last stop. He made a promise to himself to continue to learn, explore new ideas, serve the community, and remain useful and relevant.

Barth College, an excellent small liberal arts college located in Rhinebeck, often hosted concerts and performances in their Wilensky Cultural Arts Center. The Browns enjoyed the beautiful modern building and its extraordinary acoustics. They loved walking the campus and mingling with students and Hudson Valley neighbors.

Barth had recently initiated a program permitting non-matriculated learners to participate in courses at the college, either in person or virtually. There was a modest fee, of course, but the prospect of joining the young minds as a student was exciting to Andrew. He perused the Barth catalog of available classes and chose a two-semester course on the American presidency. During the first semester, they would study Washington through Woodrow Wilson, the beginning of the Depression, and World War II; then the second semester would cover Franklin Delano Roosevelt to Trump. The professor, William Fiske, was a presidential scholar of renown and chairperson of the American History Department. Andrew had met him casually at a New Year's Eve party some years ago, and found him to be friendly and engaging, with a terrific sense of humor. The class met on Tuesday and Thursday evenings from 6 to 7:30 p.m., which was perfect for Andrew's schedule. Another box checked.

The Browns had a number of close friends in Rhinebeck and the Hudson Valley, people they had known for many years, either from the University of New York, or families they had met through the children. The group was comprised of accomplished, intelligent businessmen, hospital administrators, and real estate developers of similar ages. Most importantly, the men all played golf and all were recently retired. They shared much in common, politics and a mutual disdain for Trump included. They discussed movies, books, local restaurants, and vacations.

One Saturday at lunch, Jack asked, "Does anyone have any interest in starting a book club? It could be interesting. Who knows? We might even learn something."

Initially, the suggestion was met with laughter and skepticism. But Andrew said, "Let's give it a try. We could meet monthly and have lunch—no pressure. I have an idea for the first book: *Living Cancer: Stories of an Oncologist, Father, Survivor.*"

Andrew told his friends that the author, Michael Weiner, was a colleague, a pediatric oncologist at Columbia who had written the book about his experiences caring for children with cancer and their families, as well as his own personal trials and tribulations with illness. He warned that the book was not light and carefree, but presented heart-wrenching accounts of personal human interactions.

Bruce said, "I'm game. How about you, Arthur?"

"Sure, why not?"

Andrew told Jack, Bruce, and Arthur that he would purchase *Living Cancer* for his buddies, but they said that they would download the book to their Kindles or iPads.

"Great! It's settled then. Let's meet in four weeks at the club for lunch."

All agreed. Box checked.

* * *

Andrew retained an active New York State medical license and his Bureau of Narcotics and Dangerous Drugs (BNDD) certification. Ostensibly, he could continue to practice medicine, but he lacked an integral component of patient care—malpractice insurance. What's more, there was no need for a pediatric oncologist in the Rhinebeck area.

Andrew thought about contacting Vijay Satawar, chief of pediatric oncology at Albany Medical Center, about an hour's drive to the north. But he quickly rejected the thought, having had more than enough childhood cancer in his life. Nevertheless, Brown believed he might be of use as a general pediatrician. The basic care issues such as strep throat, otitis media, diarrhea, feeding problems, and immunizations were not rocket science. He was convinced that with a little preparation, he could revert to a generalist. He decided to pursue volunteer opportunities.

After discovering that there were no available positions at the nearby hospital, Andrew called the Volunteers in Medicine America in Hudson, New York. With a little research, he'd discovered that VIM was founded by a group of retired physicians, nurses, and dentists who wanted to continue to serve their communities on a voluntary basis, providing care to those without access to health care. Since the 1990s, VIM America had built a national network of free healthcare clinics to care for the uninsured and medically underserved.

Andrew made an appointment to meet with Dr. Ranjiv Cutera, the director and physician in charge of the organization. A general practitioner in his mid-50s, Cutera had been the director of the Hudson chapter of VIM America for 11 years. He was educated in Mumbai, India and completed his residency in family medicine at Jacobi Hospital Center in the Bronx. He had a private practice in the South Bronx prior to relocating to the

Hudson Valley in search of a more tranquil environment in which to raise his family. Cutera was the only paid physician on staff. All the other providers were volunteers.

Andrew felt exhilarated as he entered Dr. Cutera's office the morning of their meeting. "I'm Andrew Brown. Pleasure to meet you, Dr. Cutera."

Andrew explained that, although he had his pediatric boards, he'd never practiced general pediatric care. "I'm confident, though, that I'll get up to speed quickly. I've already begun to relearn the basics."

Cutera laughed genially. "Not to worry. We're a bare-bones operation. No frills, but we provide a tremendous service to the underserved population of Hudson."

From his research, Andrew remembered that Hudson had an ethnically diverse population of around 30,000 people—very reasonably sized.

"There is an 80-bed general hospital in the town with a fully functioning emergency department and small intensive care unit," Cutera continued. "For more complex cases, we refer patients to either Vassar Brothers in Poughkeepsie, or the medical center in Albany. Tell me, Andrew, what were you thinking about with respect to hours?"

Andrew told Cutera that he would be comfortable beginning with two shifts, perhaps a morning and an afternoon each week. "But there is something you should know. Although my license and BNDD are active, I don't have malpractice insurance."

"No worries. VIM America has a blanket policy for all providers. When can you begin? We have open sessions for pediatrics on Monday afternoon and Thursday morning."

Community service, relevance—both boxes checked.

* * *

Andrew enjoyed spending as much time with his seven-year-old grandson as possible. He and Will were two peas in a pod. Together they shared an expression: "Us two guys driving in the car, listening to music, having a good time."

Andrew bought a set of starter golf clubs for Will—a driver, hybrid wood, three irons, and a putter, and they took every opportunity they could to go to the driving range and hit balls. Will affectionately referred to his driver as "the big dog." He seemed to have a propensity for golf, and it wasn't long before he was hitting the ball over 100 yards; not too shabby for someone so young.

But to his dismay, Andrew started to notice that Will had a temper. He was easily frustrated and would raise his voice and grit his teeth when provoked. He was prone to tantrums, and his temper was often directed toward his sister, which was not unusual but still a cause for concern. He refused to accept authority, either at home or in school, where he could be quite disruptive. Sure, there were moments of normalcy and unchallenged obedience, but his temper seemed to lurk just under the surface.

Was it possible Will had inherited the Brown anger gene? Pia was aware of her son's anger and consulted their pediatrician, but everyone agreed that it was too early to proactively attempt to alter Will's behavior. For the time being, at least, the recommendation was to monitor him closely, bring outbursts to Will's attention, ask him to calm down, and continue to observe.

The thought that inherited anger could be a part of his family legacy terrified Andrew. It troubled him deeply, but it was still too soon to tell. He knew he just had to be the best grandfather he could be and prepare Will and Clara for the future.

* * *

On balance, Andrew was content. Retirement was becoming an exciting chapter in his life. Of course, there remained the unknown variable—health. Despite attempts to maintain a positive and productive lifestyle by controlling his weight, eating healthy meals, and getting regular exercise, Andrew was more aware than most that well-being could be fleeting.

It was a cold early January morning in Rhinebeck, and the ground was frozen and covered in a monotonous blanket of white snow. Winters in the Hudson Valley could be overwhelmingly long and harsh—they required staying power. Nevertheless, Marissa and Andrew were committed to spending time at their home on Ridge Road. Although travel remained limited due to the pandemic, the Browns planned two trips to Florida—one to visit cousin Beth and her husband Mo in Boca Raton, and the second for an unveiling of the gravestone inscription, a Jewish tradition for Andrew's parents, Nathan and Ruth. In addition, they were invited to a wedding in Tucson in February. Winter would pass quickly enough.

Andrew had a busy day planned, with four Zoom calls and an interview. He took a Peloton class and showered. While shaving, he noticed a lump on the left side of his neck. It was firm and rubbery, nontender, no erythema, but the node was unmistakable—about 2 centimeters in diameter.

As a pediatric oncologist, Andrew had specialized in leukemia and lymphoma, and the most common cause for a new patient consultation was an enlarged lymph node in the neck. He had expertise in the assessment of lumps and bumps and could often make an educated diagnosis by recording the history of the present illness and physical examination. He recognized benign nodes, for which he'd recommend observation or a course of antibiotics. He was also able to ascertain lymph nodes of concern and knew when to suggest an ultrasound, chest x-ray, blood count, and a referral to a surgeon for a biopsy. If Andrew had learned anything in his more than 40-year practice, it was when there was cause for concern.

Andrew wasn't sick. In fact, he felt extremely well. He did not have any evidence of an infection—no fever, no sweating, no weight loss. It was just a lump. He told Marissa, who reacted to the revelation with calm determination. After waiting a few days, he emailed his friend, Hal Short, a surgeon, and asked if he would examine it. Short emailed back immediately and told Andrew to come to his office on the eighth floor of the Powell

Ambulatory Building at 2:30. Together, Andrew and Marissa drove to the hospital.

Hal ushered Brown into the procedure room. There was a surgical spotlight hanging from the ceiling, and glass cabinets filled with gauze and suture material, and the supplies a surgeon would need for simple ambulatory procedures lined the walls. The examination table was in the center of the room, prepped and ready.

Drs. Brown and Short were friends. They had served on similar University of New York committees, and Short had operated on Brown twice before for herniorrhaphies. Andrew trusted Hal—he was experienced, skillful, and calming.

As Andrew took a seat on the table, Dr. Short said, "Let me see that lymph node that you're concerned about."

Andrew turned his head to the left so he could see and feel the node in question.

"Well, I certainly feel what you are referring to. Is it tender? Is it bothering you at all?"

"Not really. What bothers me is that I have no explanation for its existence. I feel perfectly fine. I just want to remove it."

Short patted Andrew's shoulder and replied, "I really don't think it's anything to worry about. Let's wait a few weeks and see what happens to it."

Andrew hesitated. "Hal…my intuition tells me that you should remove it now and do the biopsy. Let's just do it. You know me. Just give me a little local lidocaine and pop it out."

Hal smiled gently. "Okay, Andrew. Take off your shirt and lie on the table with the left side of your neck up."

Dr. Short turned on the overhead surgical spotlight, removed his white coat, rolled up his sleeves, and took a sterile surgical equipment pack from the cabinet. He placed the pack unopened on a table and put on a pair of sterile gloves. When a nurse entered the room and asked if he needed assistance, he told her that he could use a hand for a few minutes. The nurse placed a sterile drape on the table and opened a pack of 4-by-4 sterile gauze. She poured betadine on the gauze and held a vial of 2 percent lidocaine so that he could withdraw the analgesic into a sterile syringe.

"Thanks, Lisette. I think I can manage from here," he said. "Before you go, though, please fill out a surgical pathology requisition form for Dr. Brown and just place a jar of Bouin's solution on the table with the top off. I'll let you know when I'm done, and if you would, I want you to hand-carry the sample to hematopathology."

Throughout, Andrew was unbothered; the procedure itself was a non-event. Regarding the anticipated result, it would be what it would be. Either way, it was beyond his control. If malignant, he figured that he'd rather know now instead of three or four weeks from now.

Brown felt Hal working diligently and deftly once the lidocaine took effect. Only a few minutes later, Hal placed the tissue in question into the bottle containing the Bouin's solution and showed it to Andrew. "Here it is—a grayish-white lymph node."

Andrew realized with a start that this 2- to 3-centimeter piece of tissue could, in some odd way, dictate his future and define his retirement. Benign or malignant, he had nothing to do now but wait.

Marissa drove home to Rhinebeck with Andrew in the passenger seat.

"You'll be fine," she reassured him. "It's probably nothing to be worried about. You have long life in your family; your father died at 95 and your mother nat 98. Don't think about it until you have to think about it."

* * *

"Andrew, you were correct," Hal told Andrew two days later. "The node is a classical low-grade follicular lymphoma."

Andrew had anticipated a diagnosis of non-Hodgkin's lymphoma. He explained that his father had diffuse large cell B-cell lymphoma diagnosed at 92 years of age and had received six cycles of aggressive chemotherapy. He lost his hair, but otherwise did incredibly well. He survived to die three years later, after a fall.

"I figured it'd be the same, so…I guess in a weird way I'm relieved."

The next step for Andrew was to choose an oncologist. The University of New York was a National Cancer Institute Comprehensive Cancer Center, and the oncology program was excellent. He knew the lymphoma doctors personally and had attended the same conferences and strategized about protocols that would bridge the gap in treatment for adolescents and young adults with hematological malignancies. They were friends and colleagues. Andrew asked Dr. Janet Amaro, a relatively new attending, to guide his care. Andrew was less concerned about therapeutic choices—he was more concerned about access, and wanted a doctor who would be a partner on his cancer journey. Dr. Amaro was perfect.

Dr. Amaro ordered a PET-CT scan and performed a bone marrow aspirate and biopsy. The latter test was normal and completely devoid of any signs of follicular lymphoma. However, the PET scan revealed several unexpected findings. There appeared to be a second positive submental lymph node consistent with follicular lymphoma. However, its location was in the same nodal region and did not represent a new anatomical area of disease, which was an excellent conclusion. But the radioactive sugar moiety used in the PET scan demonstrated an uptake in the thyroid gland. The PET also showed superficial uptake on the surface of his right upper chest wall.

Drs. Brown and Amaro met to discuss next steps. They agreed that the thyroid nodules needed to be followed and biopsied, as did the lesion on the upper chest wall. Amaro told Andrew that it would be best to clarify the other unanticipated lesions and develop an accurate diagnosis prior to initiating treatment for the lymphoma. Andrew concurred.

Andrew made appointments with Roger Briton, director of the thyroid service at the University of New York Hospital, and Laura Tedeschi, a dermatological oncologist. Briton ordered a thyroid ultrasound and biopsy, which showed papillary thyroid cancer. Tedeschi biopsied the superficial lesion—basal cell carcinoma.

Needless to say, the winter was eventful. Not one, not two, but three separate cancer diagnoses. On a Tuesday morning in February, Dr. Tedeschi did a wide excision of Andrew's basal cell carcinoma. It was successful, with free margins. The next day Hal Short performed a total thyroidectomy, margins clean, but five discrete nodules consistent with papillary carcinoma were now all extirpated. Roger Briton prescribed levothyroxine replacement therapy, but he was confident that Andrew would not need radioactive iodine ablation therapy. Next, Andrew addressed the follicular lymphoma.

Dr. Amaro prescribed a new regimen consisting of Revlimid orally, every three weeks out of four, and obinutuzumab, a stronger version of rituximab, an immunotherapy drug directed against the CD 20 antigen on the surface of lymphoma cells. Therapy was ongoing, frequent visits to the hospital for treatment. Fortunately, Andrew tolerated the treatment without toxicity or side effects. He felt neither old nor sick.

Andrew and Marissa were once again trying to enjoy retirement. Each new day now held a special significance. Life has a randomness and an unpredictable ebb and flow, but one thing that Andrew and Marissa could always rely upon was one another. No matter what the future held, they knew that they'd be able to face it head on, together.

AFTERWORD

The stories in this book are true except when they are not.

The names of all the characters have been fabricated to protect the privacy and integrity of those whom they represent.

The names of all institutions, medical centers, and demographic locations have all similarly been altered, and there is no synchrony between the characters, stories, and institutions. The University of New York and its medical school do not exist, but the politics and bureaucracy are emblematic of the author's own long career at an academic medical center.

The incidents and events are gleaned from the personal experiences and observations of the author and have been expanded upon to enhance the experience of the reader and add interest.

This is not a story that ties up neatly with a bow, because the issue it seeks to address is so nebulous and multifaceted. While readers may not always agree with Andrew Brown and may, at times, find his behavior to be abhorrent, I ultimately hope that they can relate to his desire for self-improvement and his persistence in the face of setbacks.

I also hope to shed some light on the failures of larger institutions in supporting their employees through disciplinary measures. While this book in no way seeks to validate or condone the behavior of Andrew Brown or others like him, it does demonstrate that with effort, change is possible. As the world continues to change, institutions are changing with it. Those changes are largely positive, as they allow people who have been historically marginalized to have a greater voice and increased avenues for protection in cases of inappropriate behavior and harassment. However, in doing so, they need not throw out the proverbial baby with the bathwater.

What I argue for in these pages is a more holistic and nuanced approach to correcting poor behavior in the workplace. The issues that Andrew Brown dealt with were not unique to the University of New York, nor to the medical industry more generally. Medicine has always been a clearly delineated hierarchy, and within hierarchical structures, there is an increased tendency toward abuse. That culture must change, but when institutions do not give doctors with decades of experience within one system the opportunity to adapt to a new system, they run the risk of losing valuable medical expertise and research opportunities.

I hope these pages will provide readers with an opportunity to reflect on their own behaviors and experiences—whether with anger or other emotions that may have run amuck in their own lives. And most of all, I hope that this book will serve as a road map toward personal growth.

ACKNOWLEDGEMENTS

I wish to thank Ellen Gomroy for her invaluable assistance, guidance, suggestions, and involvement from conception to completion of this book. I'd also like to thank the skilled team at Atlantic Publishing Group—Crystal Edwards, Jack Bussell, and Katie Fortuna.

I would like to recognize the significant contribution made by my family and friends. In the interest of privacy, however, many of them remain anonymous to the public.

Similarly, my real colleagues and friends at the fictitious University of New York must remain confidential. Rest assured that my sincere thanks will be conveyed personally.

ABOUT THE AUTHOR

For four decades, Michael Weiner, MD, has worked as a pediatric oncologist at a major academic medical center and prominent children's hospital in a large northeastern city. He has served as the director of pediatric oncology and as a vice chair for external affairs in the Department of Pediatrics. He has made major contributions in the diagnosis and treatment of patients with lymphoma—specifically Hodgkin's lymphoma—and has been nationally recognized as a leader in the field.

Dr. Weiner is the founder of Hope & Heroes Children's Cancer Fund, a 501(c)(3) grassroots charitable organization that supports pediatric cancer research and patient care throughout the New York, New Jersey, and Connecticut metropolitan region. He is also the executive director of DCG Giving, a charity affiliated with the Dave Cantin Group Acquisitions that provides philanthropic support to Children's Oncology Group institutions.

He has authored and edited several medical textbooks, most recently the second edition of *Secrets in Pediatric Hematology and Oncology.* He is the author of the best-selling book *Living Cancer: Stories of an Oncologist, Father, Survivor.*

CPSIA information can be obtained
at www.ICGtesting.com
Printed in the USA
JSHW031602050223
37168JS00001B/6

9 781620 239179